Tidings
From The
Abyss

70 Disturbing Micro-Dramas

David Powers

TIDINGS FROM THE ABYSS: 70 DISTURBING MICRO-DRAMAS

First Edition - August 2014

This book is a work of fiction. Names, characters, places, and incidents either are a product of the author's imagination, are used fictitiously, and any resemblance to actual persons, living or dead, business establishments, events, or locales is entirely coincidental.

Library of Congress Cataloging-in-Publication Data
Powers, David.
Tidings from the abyss: 70 disturbing micro-
dramas/David Powers.
164 p. 22 cm.

ISBN 978-0-9914248-3-2 (hardcover)
ISBN 978-0-9914248-4-9 (paperback)
ISBN 978-0-9914248-5-6 (ebook)

1. Wit and Humor. 2. United States--Social Life and Customs--
Humor. 3. Short Stories. I. Title.

Library of Congress Control Number: 2014912380
Printed in the United States of America

Eerie Forest
www.eerieforest.com

For Bob Anderson

Table of Contents

Introduction

Modern technology is exciting and constantly evolving. When voicemail was introduced to the Macy's Newark, New Jersey photographic studio in 1989, it seemed a wonderful method of exchanging amusing messages on one another's telephones.

Before long, this communication developed into a necessary diversion for me and one of the lead catalog photographers, Robert Anderson. It was always uplifting to roll in the aisles after hearing one of Bob's gut-busting yarns. Often, I would walk through Anderson's dark studio and find a group of photogs and their assistants circled around his phone laughing at one of my stupid stories. At first, the voicemails were impulsive gags that were intended to be listened to, deleted and soon forgotten. Luckily, for prosperity, we eventually decided to tape each other's messages.

Prior to leaving Haworth, New Jersey and moving to San Diego, California in 1992, I transcribed the recordings using a portable Smith Corona word processor and printed a compilation for fellow studio employees.

Reading these tales twenty-five years later, I wonder if they are now too grim or politically incorrect for contemporary human consumption. Times sure have changed with the introduction of the internet, smartphones and terrorists!

Expecting eternal condemnation from family and friends, I resurrected these potboilers, washed them off and jammed the text one more time through the meat grinder otherwise known as self-publishing.

These stories are purely fictional, and do not in *any* way reflect the ideals or philosophies of the author. Mostly, these demented notions are just things growin' in my head that need to be released. Seriously folks, these dark comedies are simply supposed to be funny!

Prom Night

ADAM POINT'S LEG TWITCHED UNCONTROLLABLY. Pinned underneath the giant Lincoln, he remembered a *Reader's Digest*, "Drama in Real Life," where a man was caught in a similar dilemma. For the life of him, Adam couldn't recall how the story ended.

A drip of gasoline hit Point's forehead, running toward his eye. The seventeen-year-old, high school senior contorted his head, the fuel rolling into an ear.

Alecia Monhesi, his prom date, stretched half in and half out of the automobile. The girl had looked gorgeous when Adam picked her up six hours ago. Alecia's parents politely greeted him in their modest living room. They stared in astonishment as Alecia descended the staircase: the Monhesi's realizing their baby had grown up and Adam in horny desire for the sexy teenager.

"Take care, kids. Adam, be safe. Lots of drunks will be on the roads tonight. And be back by midnight," cautioned the concerned father.

"Yes, Mr. Monhesi. We'll be careful," Point had responded, wrapping an arm around his date's waist.

Adam tried to see Alecia. Her bloody legs protruded through the tinted windshield.

"Alecia!" he cried, as he had been for a while now.

The adolescent knew she must be dead, but he couldn't worry about that, just yet. Adam had his own set of problems. He was thirty miles from nowhere with a two ton Lincoln Town Car crushing his femurs, tibias and fibulas.

The waxing moon illuminated the cornfields surrounding the vehicle. Eight weeks into the season and the corn soared six feet high. Fifty yards from the road, the car's tire tracks led back to the scorched skids where Point swerved to avoid the dawdling opossum.

No one would find them until daybreak. That might be too late. Adam's legs were split (resembling boiled Sabrett's hotdogs) and spilled cooling body fluids onto the black earth.

"God, oh God!" he pleaded to the empty cornfields. "Please help me!"

Of course, nobody heard Adam Point.

Seth Jenkins snaked his way into the field, heading toward the secret hiding place. The corn grew very tall, over nine feet high and almost ready for market. Jenkins worried what might happen at harvest time.

The schoolboy had carefully memorized the route. The point of entrance was a drainage ditch. Walking twenty rows into the corn, he followed the column another seventy-five feet.

The holy sanctuary inspired Seth. After school, he had created the site by ripping out hundreds of cornstalks to form a perfect circle. Jenkins was dying to tell his friends, but he knew he couldn't. This was too important to goof-up. Patrick or Jaxon might inform their parents and then he'd get in big trouble. It was none of their damn business anyway.

Seth crossed into his sacred place from the same spot each time, a small knoll with the best vantage point. The four-door sedan remained on four wheels, although flat now. Jenkins viewed the female—he had studied her closely. The male lay squashed under the chrome door sill running between the front and rear tires. Brother Adam (he had pulled the wallet and scrutinized the license) was the "Screamer." The dried-out husk's face grimaced, as if in incredible pain. The girl remained a mystery.

Seth reverently approached the altar. The shrine was a 1987 Ford Lincoln Town Car, pearl with burgundy interior. Shaped like a humongous refrigerator, the navy-blue vinyl top gave the automobile regal definition. The boxy grill shined chromed magnificence, and the spoked wheels remained dazzling in the midafternoon sun. Fully-loaded, the whale was a capitalist's dream car.

Jenkins respectfully readied himself by removing his T-shirt, shorts, and underpants before entering the circle. He left his sneakers on, preferring not to step on any sharp stones or insects.

"Mecca Lecca High Mecca Hiney Ho," the squat, ninth-grader intoned, closing his eyes. "I give Brother Adam and Sister Eve to you, Oh Great Corn God!"

Seth observed this ritual for weeks with no verifiable results. In frustration, he leapt onto the roof of the awe-inspiring heap of Detroit iron.

The nude boy began the incantation, "Open Sesame! Abracadabra! Hocus Pocus-Hocus Pocus!" while capering upon the great white hulk.

The car bounced, the beehive jounced, and of course fell off. Five hundred thousand angry africanized bees swarmed onto the amateur warlock.

Fly Free

EUGENE SQUINTED at the image reflected in the steamy glass of the bathroom mirror.

"Superman!" Eugene screeched and weakly flexed. His hollow grin displayed rows of useless teeth. "I better go to a dentist," he worried, wiggling a decayed ivory with a finger.

Eugene critically evaluated the sickly individual glaring back. "I've really let myself go," he wheezed, rank breath causing him to retreat.

The rodent exterminator noticed a row of spots, starting from his left ear and ending at the outie belly button. They resembled normal white-heads: red mountains crowned with snowy peaks. Eugene absently picked at a bump below his nipple. The spot burst, releasing a fine-grain powder resembling brown sugar.

"Jesus," he murmured, examining the opening more closely. The hissing blemish now revealed a hole in his chest cavity. The ratman scratched manically at the perforation. Piece by piece, he tore small strips of flesh from his breast. It didn't hurt much. The skin felt as dry and crispy as the tissue paper covering a child's model airplane. Pulling faster, the protective shell parted. *There it was!* Eugene's heart pulsed rapidly, flapping within his ribcage, not unlike a trapped bird.

"Fly free, fly free," he grunted, grabbing a bone and yanking it clear. The heart was now only loosely tethered by dusty and cracked arteries. "Fly free my pretties!"

Eugene plucked the shriveled sack from between his ribs and promptly fell over dead.

Detective Amy

AMY TORREZ'S BOOTS squished on the bloody staircase. The fluids oozed and coagulated on the shag carpet—the walls splattered Jackson Pollock-style. It appeared as if a massacre had occurred here at the Baker residence. Up the stairs Amy went. She was a detective after all and exposed to every kind of mayhem.

The master bedroom contained the bodies of a married couple (she could determine this by the matching wedding rings). Lying supine on the bed and holding hands, Paula and George Baker's skulls were shattered. *"Shotgun?"* Torrez wondered, as her stomach did a rolling flip-flop, ready to disgorge. She did not however and continued the search.

The children's bedroom held the remains of the two Baker daughters—violent crimson stains soaking the sheets. A baseball bat, the grip smeared with bloody handprints lay amongst the fuzzy teddy bears. Pulling on latex gloves, Amy gulped at this horror show.

Grandma Trevor, Paula Baker's mother, resided in the guest bedroom. The poor woman sat in a rocking chair, skinned like a Florida orange. Torrez slumped against the doorframe. *Lord, a whole family murdered!*

With more of the premises to search, Amy checked the hallway closet. Ned, the family dog, stuck to the inside of the door, his fur matted with hot glue.

"Ugh!" Detective Torrez choked. Nuggets of baloney sandwich sweetened with bile sauce leapt up her esophagus. Gripping the flashlight, she kept it together.

A light flickered from a room in the corridor—the bathroom. Inside, slumped on the toilet sat Grandpa Trevor, a *Popular Science* magazine swinging from one hand. Disemboweled, his guts dripped into the bowl. Amy wanted to flush but didn't. The academy trained her to not alter any evidence. Reeling, she left the lavatory.

Out the hall window, she saw the nude corpses of Grandma Baker and Grandpa Baker obscenely wired to the children's jungle gym.

"God help them. God help me!" Torrez sobbed. Grimly, she continued her investigation.

A door accessed the attic. Amy climbed the narrow wooden stairs. Fumbling as she found the switch, a splinter stuck her hand, drawing a red dot. The loft was recently painted maroon, or so she originally thought. Blood coated these walls, not Benjamin Moore paint—gallons too, by the looks of it. There were no victims up here, solely lots of gore. Detective Amy descended feeling very lost.

As Torrez returned to the second floor hallway, she nearly tripped over the maid, a Scandinavian gal working her way to American citizenship. The clothesline wrapped around the woman's throat sliced deeply into the folds of her neck.

Amy drew her service revolver. The killer could still be in the house—she'd recheck the upper level.

Into the bathroom she went, the pistol cocked. Grandpa Trevor now unfolded across the black and white-tiles. A dozen ultra-sharp steak knives protruded from his ribs. A meat cleaver glinted next to the elderly man's carved up buttocks.

The hall closet remained ajar. Ned's torso lay in a hamper. His collar and head were missing.

Detective Amy burst into the Baker daughters' bedroom. The bed had been stripped, the mattress wet with escaping life. A trail of blood led to the pink flowery curtains and out the window. Panting, she raced to the sash. Stuffed in metal garbage cans, five-year-old Ashlee and seven-year-old Janice blazed in black clouds of gasoline smoke. Elfin slippers on splayed legs pointed upwards.

Torrez's clenched hand rose to her mouth. *She must not lose control of this situation!* Gun shaking, she haltingly crawled to Grandma Trevor's bedroom. At first nothing seemed changed. The old woman's body still resembled a peeled Valencia—all messed up. When Amy rolled the stiffening carcass on her back, she noticed the difference—Ned's head was stapled onto Grandma's neck!

"Where is the old woman's head?" she moaned.

Detective Amy carefully entered the hallway. Revisiting the master bedroom, spongy grey matter coated her shoes. The parents lay prostrate—the skulls' interiors picked clean. A shiny sphere rolled inside Paula Baker's head. "A glass eyeball," she gasped.

Torrez heard a muffled thumping coming from somewhere below. Springing, she charged to the stairway, slipped on fatty tissue and fell down the steps breaking her spine.

As Detective Amy flickered in and out of consciousness, she listened to Grandma Trevor's head thumping in the family's brand-new Maytag gas dryer.

The Hole

PROPPED BY THE SHOVEL, Lincoln mopped his brow. Jesus, it was hot as hell. Thinking of better places to be, he looked around the backyard.

"Donny, what are you doing? We're not done yet. The sooner you dig this hole, the sooner you can go play with your friends," Max, Lincoln's father grunted, breaking the silence of the humid August afternoon.

Gnats buzzed into Lincoln's ear. Impatiently, he swatted the pests away. He hated working with his dad. The old man always created a big job out of every project and used his son for slave labor. Scowling, the boy pried at a stubborn root with the spade.

Gradually, the crater took shape.

Lincoln had awoken that dawn to his mother's urgent whoops. "Max, Max! The laundry tub is overflowing! Hurry!"

Out of curiosity, the teenager padded to the basement. There in the gloom, his sleepy senses were assaulted with the unsettling sights, sounds and smells of his parents mopping up buckets of pasty black sludge. Evacuating in disgust, he quietly crept upstairs and returned to bed.

Blanket overhead, Lincoln planned his Saturday activities. First, he would enjoy an overflowing bowl of Sugar Pops while reading cartoons. After a leisurely bike ride to the seedy side of town to buy cheap Mexican brick weed from Cricket, he might wander over to Woody's and spend the day getting high. The adolescent sighed with contentment, floating away to never-never land.

"Donny, rise and shine. We've got work to do!" his pa blared, pushing into the bedroom. "Wear your old clothes—you're gonna get dirty. Meet me in the kitchen in five minutes."

"Oh man," the tired teen groaned. He pulled on wrinkled trousers, a sleeveless shirt and his new kicks.

His father bore a resemblance to General Patton planning an important invasion as he studied the drawing on the kitchen table. Max wore his Viet Nam sweats—not a good sign.

"Come here. I want you to focus on this." The diagram was an architect's view of his yard. A fat "X" marked the middle. It was where the grass was the greenest and grew the highest. "This here's the septic tank. I guess it's plugged. Have you been using too much toilet paper, Son?" Lincoln's dad accused, with narrowed blood-shot eyes.

"Uh, no sir. I just use little clumps." Lincoln's face reddened as he scratched his butt.

"Well, no matter. We gotta dig the mother up. Go put on your old sneakers and meet me outside. Bring a couple of shovels." His father rose abruptly, sending the chair slamming into the dishwasher. The General stomped out of the house.

As Lincoln switched shoes, he cursed his misfortune.

Forty-eight minutes later, Max hit concrete. The pair used their hands to scrape the fertile earth from the septic tank. Father and son peered into the ground.

"Okay, Donny. I'll pry and you pull. It's gonna smell like a stank-hole, but it won't kill you. Put these rubber gloves on."

Max jammed the pry bar under the lid and put his back into the task. The cover came up easily, exposing the cesspool. Three feet by six feet, the cistern overflowed with brown effluent. Latex condoms and plastic tampon applicators manned by mutinying insect crews sailed across the surface.

"Hmmm. What a mess, huh Donny? Well, the quicker we find the clog, the sooner we can wash up." Max grabbed the shovel, deftly probing the oily sewage. "There's stuff down there alright. Let's see what it is." He spat into the wastewater and stirred the swill.

Dipping the tool, Max ladled the debris. Gingerly, he tipped the spade to the side and drained off the liquid. The curve of the scoop displayed a mishmash of digits: toes and fingers.

"Balls!" Lincoln's father cursed. "Your mom's up to her old tricks again!" Face ruddy with fury, Max dropped the shovel and rushed into the house to confront his wife.

Vinnie Goes Bad

VINNIE RUSSO SINNED A LOT LATELY. In and out of trouble since the tender age of sixteen; Vinnie was bad. At nineteen, he wound up in a minimum security penal institution in the red state of Louisiana.

The young man got there by bonking a poor grocer on the head with a juicy watermelon. The elderly victim positively identified Russo as the assailant.

Vinnie's first day in prison was pretty lousy. Gang raped three times in a twenty-four hour period leaves a lasting impression on an innocent lad. That night, as Russo sniveled with great pain into the stained pillow, he vowed never to be violated again.

The next sunup, reborn, Vinnie poked a fellow jailbird in the eye with a hard piece of crust secreted from dinner. The man yelped and screaked as he extracted the crumbs from reddening eyes. Russo was crowned King of Cell Block G. The other felons, even the rapists and perverts, looked upon Vinnie as a leader of men.

Vinnie made many important decisions that year. In one controversial case, two inmates claimed custody of a rat designated either "Skip" or "Felix" depending on who retained the animal. Judge Russo searched his bible school notes and declared a ruling. He sliced the pet in half, each prisoner given a chance to flip for the rat's head. The man who named the rodent Skip won the toss. Later, he paraded around the prison yard with Skippy's skull stuck upon a Popsicle stick.

As I mentioned earlier, Vinnie succumbed to temptation often. On a daily basis, the miscreant tackled breaking the Ten Commandments. The single principle he failed to taint was the directive prohibiting adultery. The problem was that there were no married couples in the penitentiary.

Vinnie pondered and wondered, finally working out a plan. On Sundays, Father O'Leary preached at the prison chapel. Everyone said the priest was married to God. Russo knew what he had to do.

"You look nice today, Father," Vinnie complimented, raising his voice up a notch. "Very nice indeed."

Ali Comes to America

ALI CROUCHED IN THE SHRUBS behind Burger King, ready to strike.

"I've been branded a thief, so I might as well be a thief," he thought, legs tightly coiled and ready to spring.

Bored waiting for his victim, Ali's mind returned to the crossing—quite pleasant in fact. It was hot and the murky water of the Rio Grande cooled his skin as he backstroked to America.

Before Ali had tearfully left his family, Libyan friends deported from the United States taught him the language. "Get a job pumping gas. In America," they explained, "there is an Exxon station on every corner. The only words of English you'll need to remember are: 'Fill 'er up?' and 'Have a nice day!'"

Ali had no problem landing the job. In advance to approaching the station manager, the immigrant liberally soaked his coveralls in gasoline and engine oil. His initial customer drove a rusty Jeep Scrambler.

"Fill 'er up?" Ali asked the spaced-out Yankee.

"Ten dollars of the regular," the bearded driver requested.

The gas station attendant stuck the nozzle into the tank, swishing the fuel around while counting, *"Wahid, Ithnaan, Thalaatha."* After hanging up the hose and screwing the cap onto the Jeep, he approached the driver's window and parroted, "Ten dollars of the regular."

"Ten dollars?" the driver responded in disbelief. The pump's gauge had only advanced to fifty-three cents.

Smiling, Ali took the cash. "Have a nice day." He jammed the bills down his pants—one for the boss and nine for himself. Gleefully drawing on a king-size Chesterfield, the crook exclaimed, "This is easy!"

Later that afternoon, after getting fired, Ali developed the concept for the Burger King heist. Along came the perfect victim: a horned gentleman of indeterminate age carrying a greasy bag of onion rings.

"Ten dollars!" Ali shouted at the now fuming, Prince of Darkness.

Boy's Room

WORRIED, TERRENCE RODRIGUEZ TAPPED A FOOT. At his cramped school desk, he shifted restlessly in the attached chair. Rodriguez's intestines lurched with each click of the second hand on the big clock. The teacher droned endlessly about the Neapolitan Revolution.

The boy's thoughts drifted back to lunch hour. As usual on Wednesdays, the school cafeteria served his favorite: eggplant lasagna. The schoolboy scarfed the pasta alone, for he had no friends, unless you counted Weenie, a mute kid with a patchy crew cut.

Now Terrence squirmed in pain—the kind that got worse just before an important organ ruptured. Five more minutes remained until class ended, so he internally distracted himself solving quadratic equations; but to no avail. Rodriguez had to go bad.

Pushing the eyeglasses up his nose, Terrence planned his actions. After the teacher closed with the usual, "Don't forget to complete your homework," he would escape to the busy hallway. Rodriguez knew where the boy's room was, but had never been inside. He always went home to his safe pastel toilet. The youth was afraid to use the lavatory at school. Several times, he had overheard that horrible things happened in there: drugs, cigarettes and dirty talk. Terrence held his bowels until he got home, often running all the way to his apartment building.

At long last, the bell rang. Rodriguez scrambled to his feet and bolted to the exit, clutching his Star Trek book bag. Outside, the hall was pandemonium: children laughing, swearing and slamming lockers. The young man determinedly walked along the hallway as kids poked him with pencils and rulers. Unwilling to shit himself, the stocky lad put an arm straight out and slammed the door open. Now a big boy, Terrence could deal with whatever waited.

Need creates determination!

The crowd in the darkened lavatory swiveled when their nerdy classmate barged in. For an instant, the dank chamber was deathly quiet as the group realized their good fortune.

"Hey four-eyes," Peter Pussy sputtered. "What are you doing here? Looking to suck off Weenie?"

Everyone hooted and hollered at that—it was kind of funny. Rodriguez hesitated, then courageously pulled his head high and shuffled toward a toilet. Halfway in the stall, Peter Pussy grabbed his collar, tearing the polo shirt in the process.

"Hey four-eyes, hey four-eyes!" the throng chanted.

After the punching began, a violent chain reaction followed. Terrence voided himself as he hit the grimy, green-tiled floor.

The mob punched and kicked until they heard the warning, "Principal Turner's coming!" Furtive as moles, the riffraff vanished. Rodriguez lay in a puddle of blood and excrement, sobbing into what remained of his sleeve.

"Who did this Terrence?" the principal asked. "I need to know."

"Well, Peter Pussy started it, but the Big Greek and the Crazy Swede joined in too. Then some other guys that are older than me!" the youngster cried.

"Son, we'll make those bastards pay," the petite man swore.

Out in the Bush

THE WORDS CAME TO HIM CLEARLY NOW. "You got to say what you got to say, don't you?"

The camper stood on top of the picnic table, very drunk. "Eat me!" he caterwauled into the chilly night. Gazing into the heavens, the smog test technician danced and sang, "Twinkle, twinkle little star, how I wonder what you are!"

The moon was full, or close enough, he thought, howling. Life had been a joke up to this point, with no immediate chance for change. Swaying, the man raised the frosty can of Budweiser Dry and cursed, "Fuck you! FUCK YOU!" The White Label-laced beer coursed through his arteries.

The smogman whirled, squinting into the darkness. "Who's there?" he called. "Who the fuck's out there?"

There was no answer. No one gave a fuck, about the fucker, out there in the bush.

Chastity

NAMED BY HER HIPPY PARENTS DURING A WEEKEND ACID TRIP, Chastity was now a full-grown woman with many emotional hang-ups.

Her mother, a popular media slut with a surgically enhanced body, had mentally abused the girl when she was younger.

Chastity's father, currently the mayor of Detroit, had also physically battered the child after signing her report cards.

So now in the prime of life, Chastity, a voluptuous brunette with an award winning set of incisors, brought it upon herself to wear a diamond-studded, gold-plated, Proctor Silex chastity belt, along with various other unwieldy protection devices.

Birth, Rebirth and Decay

AS I DRAGGED MYSELF across the buckled linoleum toward the dishwasher, my discarded legs twitched in a shadowy corner of the kitchen. Lying sideways and craning my neck, I discerned the fuzzy shape of a swollen anaconda nesting under the refrigerator. Against my ear, the unrelenting humming of high voltage motors masked the crying babies growing in the basement. Distraught, I desperately tried to recall any of the infant's names. Wriggling onto my spine, bits of broken glass ground into my shoulder blades. My eyes spiraled followed the revolving fan hanging from the tin ceiling.

An athletic man entered the gymnasium, a basketball in one hand and a football clenched under his arm. "Which is yours?" he asked, the mustache topping two rows of corncob. I had no idea.

In the auditorium, my legs made an appearance atop the brilliant stage. The pants danced, as if controlled by a drunken puppeteer. Searching for the magic, I glimpsed the cables and fish hooks.

"Please don't allow my limbs to dry out!" I pleaded to the director.

A loud chorus of angelic singing erupted as extraordinarily long walking canes pulled the wobbly legs aside.

Suffering deep loss and sadness, I sobbed, the spotlights illuminating my face. “Take me!” I shouted, wishing to be understood by the intelligentsia.

When the cheering died, I still heard the giant direct current motors spinning endlessly beneath the floorboards.

Sightless eyes blinking, the babies waited impatiently for their milk maidens.

Vinnie Wakes Up

VINNIE RUSSO AWOKE to another sunshiny Las Vegas morning. Something felt strange—something felt a matter. Last night remained a total blank. He vaguely recollected squeezing into chinos, then heading out to Club Rhino on the Strip.

"Christ, why can't I remember? Did I blackout?"

Russo wandered to the master bathroom. Pissing a golden river, he belched and farted. Hungry and hung-over, Vinnie trudged to the kitchen. High-tech and spotless, the appliances gleamed blazing white. In the sink, the sunlight sparkled off the scarlet serrated edge of a long bread knife.

"Oh, Jesus," he murmured. "Not again."

Vinnie hunted for the body. Once he found a girl in the backyard strapped to the swamp cooler, her naked torso ripped to shreds. Another time, a hooker swung from a meathook in the attic. The drug-fueled escapades blended into fading visions of torrid sex and violent murder. A more thorough search would have to take place after breakfast.

L'eggo my Eggos with real Vermont maple syrup would do the trick. Russo opened the icebox, amazed to find dozens of stacked packages, each neatly wrapped in wax paper and nicely sealed with tape. Everything was labeled. Vince sorted through the fresh bundles: arms, hands, legs. They were all there—*or were they?*

Timothy's Head a Growin'

IT WAS HARD for Timothy Dutton to think that far back. Over a year ago, the changes began slowly, but grew steadily. He seemed to recall that the earliest symptoms of the abnormality were first noticed at a New York Mets baseball game in the spring of 1990. A painful headache escalated midway through the third inning, so Timothy removed the cheap souvenir Mets cap. The hatband that once clamped his head securely, now squeezed tight as an oil filter wrench. Stretching the hat, Dutton realized that the adjustable plastic band was in the next to the last spot. The sports fan opened the hoop to the final notch and replaced the hat on his melon.

"My head's, a gettin' bigger," Timothy joked to his bewildered friends.

During the next few weeks, as the backhoe operator trenched out new sewer lines, Dutton had the uncanny sensation that, yes, his head was a growin'.

Timothy studied himself in the mirror. The head didn't appear much bigger to the naked eye, but the Mets hat no longer fit. In fact, the blue cap resembled a child's toy perched atop his thinning hair. The worried laborer leaned closer and touched the pitted glass. His complexion was very dry and stretch marks etched across the jagged cheekbones.

The Stanley tape measure wrapped around his head recorded a startling fact. Timothy's head now had a circumference of twenty-seven inches.

Each morning, Dutton measured his forehead and charted the data. Eighteen days later, the shocked trencher acknowledged it was time to make an appointment with his family doctor. The dome was growing at the alarming rate of two inches per week.

Doctor Pike paused and focused on the young man. He conducted an extensive checkup using calipers, rulers, and protractors. The doctor rubbed his nose and sighed. Pike had no theory on what was wrong with his patient. Now and again the head did enlarge. This was usually caused by hydrocephalus, otherwise known as "water on the brain."

This was obviously not hydrocephalus. *Uh, uh, no way!*

The medical books (footnotes referencing *Guinness Book of World Records*) stated that the largest head ever recorded in modern history was twenty-nine and three-quarters around. The baleful soul on the examination table exhibited a noodle with a girth of thirty-two inches!

Doctor Pike sent the freaky-looking kid home with a promise. "Timothy, we'll get to the bottom of this. Just stay calm, don't lose your head. My assistant will schedule you for more tests. Please don't forget to follow my instructions. The treatment might help and surely cannot hurt."

Stunned, Timothy left the doctor's office. Nauseous, he felt numb—he had been sure Doctor Pike would be able to help get rid of this elephantine noggin.

Dutton maneuvered into his tiny Datsun and drove to a drug store to buy the supplies the doctor prescribed. The pharmacist gawked as he laid the purchases on the counter.

"Nice weather, huh?" the squirrelly pill pusher inquired, trying to see if the monstrosity could talk.

"Yeah, wonderful," Timothy responded, restraining tears.

In his studio apartment, the ditch digger prepared the poultice. Delicately grinding the rare herbal ingredients together, Timothy revisited his disastrous date last week with the cute girl at the end of the hall. Ginny had not seen him since his head started a growin'. When Dutton arrived to pick up the young lady, his skull hardly fit in the door.

"Help me, please!" Timothy's mammoth mouth whined, to no one in particular.

MPG

SHAWN WAS A VISIONARY. The nine-year-old dreamed of invention. The boy was a tinkerer who excelled in combining this and that into wild and wonderful innovations. His father, a geek himself, provided his son with an efficient work space equipped with every tool imaginable. A computer controlled the helpful gizmos executing otherwise mundane tasks.

The schoolboy sat on a stool, contemplating his latest creation. Last week, he presented the science project to his third grade class. The device was a fist-sized carburetor that could easily get one hundred and fifty miles to the gallon on regular gasoline. As Shawn charted how to get more distance out of the sucker, he didn't know that his classmate Chad Tannenbaum had told his dad about the carb. Mr. Tannenbaum worked for an international oil conglomerate.

The side door of the garage slammed open. Shah Garuby and his bodyguard Abdul marched into the room.

"Where's the carb?" the Shah asked.

"What?" Shawn managed to stutter.

"Is this it?" Abdul lisped, pointing to a shiny object under the florescent glare. The thug picked up the gadget and fondled the tubes before sticking the artificial heart in his backpack.

"And we need the plans too," Shah Garuby ordered.

"But I haven't got any plans!" Shawn squawked. The budding genius kept his ideas deep inside his brain.

"Yeah right. Abdul, get that beagle."

The henchman lumbered across the spotless grey floor to Spot's cozy bed. The pup squealed excitedly as Abdul lifted the animal and carried it to his master.

"We'll ask you again, kid. Where are the papers?" the Shah questioned.

Shawn's eyes widened as the heartless Saudi Arabians each grabbed a kicking canine leg and prepared to make a wish. Crazy with fear, the youth blubbered.

Snapping puppy joints are loud, but not as deafening as the shrieks that pierced the night.

The experimenter awoke from his stupor and grabbed the prototype phaser pistol. He wasn't sure if the weapon would work, for after all, Shawn was only a stripling, not even pubic yet. The inventor took aim at Shah Garuby and squeezed the plastic trigger. Charging, the converted toy buzzed and hissed. The youngster's eyes burned as the blue-green ray leapt from the gun.

Special note to dog lovers: Not to worry! The young inventor developed the phaser with three settings: Instant Death, Instant Healing and Off. Shawn mended Spot's broken limbs before claiming the Nobel Prize in Physics. Both now live happily in Waco, Texas.

Ghost on Steve

UNABLE TO MOVE, Steve's eyes bulged in terror. A ghost sat upon his chest—a good-sized one too. Trapped, his body sank into the mattress.

This is exactly what Steve had been afraid would happen. Several nights ago, over dinner at a fancy Portuguese restaurant, he had originally learned of sleep paralysis. Apparently, under certain circumstances, it was possible to be caught unaware by a malevolent spirit. The occupant of the bed might awake, barely able to breathe or maneuver arms and legs.

The frightened mechanic tried to flex his knees to push the invisible force away. *Impossible!* Steve then shoved upwards with his elbows. No luck.

"Damn," the prisoner thought. "I'm going to be late for work. Jed will kill me!"

Steve found it possible to twist his neck slightly as if swimming through molasses. Unable to turn his eyes, he angled his head to see the telephone.

"How can I make a call when I can't even wiggle my hands or feet?" Steve recalled the claustrophobic feeling he regularly had beneath a car while working on the chassis. He must find a way out from underneath the duppy.

Steve sought to identify the entity, only seeing his dresser across the bedroom. Sighing, he was at a loss for what to do.

The grease monkey strained to remember what his friend Loren had recited regarding the heavy ghosts. *Some gibberish about kissing?* Could it be that he had to kiss the ghost, much as a girl may smooch a toad to release the prince? No. *This must not be so!*

Steve had grown up with limited physical contact from either of his parents and found intimacy especially unsettling. *There ought to be another method to exorcise the demon forever!*

The mechanic knew he had to act hastily, for it was becoming increasingly difficult to gasp for air. Kissing did involve saliva. Maybe the actual act of osculating was not necessary. Might the effects of the spittle (a viscid acid) drive the banshee away?

"I've got to do something soon. Can spitting on a ghost be harmful?" Steve wondered as he cleared his throat.

Jacob's Dead Plane

SOMETHING SPUN HIGH IN THE SKY—*an unidentified flying object?* Happening upon a bow and arrow, I sent a long, thin spear into the clouds. The spinning bird fell, careening wildly into the forest behind my aunt's cottage.

"Hey there!" A familiar boy entered the yard by squeezing between the missing slats in the picket fence. The lad clutched (the fingers sheathed with gold gypsy rings) an upside-down model airplane. The arrow protruded from the plane's body and the bent landing gear resembled curled claws. "My plane," he spoke accusingly. "You killed Inanna."

"So sorry, Jacob," I mumbled, my face hot. The youth hovered in a trancelike state, his eyes rarely blinking. "I'll fix your toy," I promised, pulling the delicate balsawood model from his grasp.

Cradling the hurt airship, I trotted to my aunt's kitchen. In haste, I searched the room from top to bottom for a tube of airplane cement, only discovering a bottle of solidified boat adhesive.

"Aunty! Aunty Barbara!" I shouted. There was no reply.

Frowning, I placed the wreckage on the cutting board and went upstairs. Carnal groans echoed from below my aunt's bedroom door. Lying with my cheek pressed to the floor, I peeked through the gap.

Satyr Xavier stood astride Aunt Barbara. The naked woman appeared rapturous or unconscious or both.

"Satyr Xavier," I whispered into the crack, not wanting to disturb my aunt. Part hominid, but mostly goat, the deity turned toward the door.

"It is me, Satyr Xavier. Down here!" I called a smidge louder. "Do you know where the airplane glue is? I need to fix Jacob's crop-duster."

"Shush up," the anthropomorphic battering ram hissed, dropping to his knees. "Come back later. Come back tomorrow. Don't come back at—"

I didn't wait to hear the rest and went downstairs to the basement.

The cellar was very cluttered and disorganized. Dim light filtered through water-spotted casements. A squat, balding man bent over an artist's table, a magnifier placed before his eye. Uncle Anthony studied a squirming cockroach pinned to a blueprint.

"Excuse me, Uncle Anthony. I seem to have accidentally broken Jacob's plane and need airplane glue to repair it. I can't find any in the house," I said anxiously. The hour was getting dangerously late.

"These ugly bastards are intriguing," my uncle squeaked, his artificial larynx howling with feedback. "Can you fathom that the ancestors of this teeny bug were around when dinosaurs stalked this wild planet?" The entomologist prepared to scorch the insect with a blow torch.

Ignored, I returned to the kitchen and examined my project. Colored indigo, the aircraft had yellow streaks under the broken wings. The plastic propeller was snapped in three places. Ingeniously hidden inside, a rubber band provided power. The toy was restorable, but I felt driven to smash it to pieces anyhow.

Deep in guilt, the ringing doorbell startled me.

"Who is it?" I asked nervously, appreciating full well who it was.

"It's Jacob. Where's my plane? You should have fixed Inanna and you better have done it right!" the big-man-in-a-little-boy's-body roared.

Inhaling, I opened the screen and held out a brown paper bag containing the hundreds of airplane pieces.

"I had a bit of trouble fixing your plane," I moaned, watching him reach into his knapsack.

"That's a shame," Jacob said, readying the potato peeler.

War Talk

A SPECK OF DIRT irritated Gene's eyeball. "Jesus," he whined, rubbing at the tear duct with the back of a sticky hand.

"What's your problem, Puss Boy?" Crow asked, his smudged face glaring from the next foxhole.

"Nothing man. I just got crud in my eye," Gene replied. He pulled on the eyelash, increasing the soreness. The soldier wished he had brought Visine and considered using his canteen to wash out the oculus, but changed his mind. Fresh water was too precious to waste.

A cawing blackbird swooped kamikaze-style into the brush. The platoon had bivouacked in the "Forbidden Zone" for thirty-six hours.

"What are we waiting for?" Gene wondered.

Earlier, Sergeant Chaten hinted at their mission. "Gentlemen, we're gonna do some killin'. Blood is gonna spill! Jesus, fuckin' Christ, someone's got to die!" the excited Sergeant yelled. "So get yourself ready with God 'cause we're gonna do some killin'!"

Gene's throat tightened at such talk. Six weeks ago, the young man had joined the army to get an education and not to murder or be murdered.

Luckily, the rural high school that Gene graduated from offered the stranded seniors an opportunity to leave the narrow-minded Peoria, Ohio suburb. The majority of the union jobs at the factories and grain mills were long gone. That left pumping gas or hanging around the snack machines at the unemployment office.

The sign had looked appealing to the straight D student. The poster depicted a soldier in a camouflaged uniform, his grinning face darkened with war paint. One hand clutched an American flag, while the other raised a battered M16 rifle in victory. "Today's Army Wants to Join You!" was printed in bold letters underneath this rousing photograph.

That sure sounded great to Gene, who had never ventured outside of the Buckeye State in his eighteen boring years of life. "What can I lose?" he wondered.

The balding Army recruiter was very nice to Gene, offering him a soda pop and one of "my wife's delicious homemade brownies." Lowering himself behind the big mahogany desk, he questioned, "Why do you want to join us, son?" The hypnotic eyes never left his subject.

"Well, my father died several years ago, and it's been awful hard on my mother trying to make ends meet," the pimply youngster blurted, releasing the pressure of a thousand sleepless nights. "Mom wants more for me than she had growing up. Always taking care of my grandma, she didn't even get a chance to graduate high school. I want to go to college—it doesn't matter what for. Maybe engineering, I don't know. I gotta leave the Midwest, sir," Gene wept.

"Son, I see that you're the type of man that can do the job," the Lieutenant praised. Slurping sweetened coffee, he smiled. They were all the same, these naive hayseeds. "Please sign these forms and we'll notify you."

Soon, Gene received papers in the mailbox informing him to come in for a physical and psychological exam. The senior passed both with flying colors and was bussed to the boot camp at Fort Benning.

Now, he was deep in the Georgian forest preparing to kill.

"Crow, what's happening?" Gene asked the other soldier.

"Shut up, Puss Boy!" Crow hissed. "If Chaten hears us talking, we're dead meat. Got it?" The GI returned to endlessly scanning the hillside.

What is this Forbidden Zone and why is the Sergeant acting so crazy? These were a few of the troubling thoughts revolving through the confused boy's head. "Merely part of a drill," Gene concluded.

"Sarge!" Grant, a towering southerner called urgently. "Op-position at ten o'clock!" The trooper forked his eyes downhill.

The forty-two man rifle platoon swung to view a twosome of hikers trudging up a path toward the ambush.

"Follow my initiative," Sergeant Chaten commanded, his malevolent eyes gleaming. "Blowser, you and Grant remain here. Mantly, Barstol, Evens, and Wilson, go beyond that stand of fir and wait for my signal. The rest of you stick to my heels. We're gonna catch those motherfuckers red-handed!"

Gene followed Crow as they noiselessly flanked the hikers. He didn't comprehend what was going on, but he had been taught to obey orders. The team huddled close to the sergeant below a crest of rock hidden to the approaching civilians. Lying on his belly, the recruit covertly observed the pair. A male in his early twenties joked with a younger female. Gene's eyes were drawn to the woman. Angelic, the lass' blonde hair bounced in a braided ponytail. Raising a water bottle, she smiled at something her partner said.

"That's crazy," the girl giggled. The raw cacophony of automatic weapons fire split the stillness. Gene whipped his head to catch the sergeant rise, the machinegun bucking wildly as he shot from the hip. Bullets arced into the male hiker.

"Fucker! Eat this!" Sergeant Chaten hollered as the backpacker collapsed on the trail. "And fuck that horse you rode in on!"

The young lady kneeled in shock before her companion. Suddenly she started screaming.

"Shut the fuck up!" Sergeant Chaten bellowed, quickly reloading. Training the gun on the unhinged teenager he directed, "Shoot the insurgent. Let's go! Nail the bitch!"

With a war cry, the whole platoon fired. In seconds, the woman's body turned into liver pate as the M16s cut her in half.

Gene beheld his smoking rifle, the metal of the barrel sizzling hot. He too had killed the girl, although he didn't actually remember pulling the trigger. Checking the firearm's magazine, the soldier realized it was empty. Gene felt better after reloading.

"Well done gentlemen. Let's get showers and chow back at camp," Sergeant Chaten said, examining the dead for gold teeth. "I believe Cookie's got pork and beans tonight."

Spoiled

THE MASHED POTATOES appeared tainted to Carl Rawlings, but he ate them nevertheless. He was hungry.

For the last fortnight, everything tasted awful to the confused electrician. The fruit was rotten, the hamburger smelled and looked off. Those chicken breasts had to be loaded with salmonella and the milk that Carl poured on the cereal this morning made him instantly spit the Cheerios onto the linoleum. The milk must have turned sour and putting his nose to the "V" in the cardboard carton, the insidious fermentation was obvious. *Curdled.* That was a word that made you sick just saying it.

Rawlings checked the refrigerator every few hours. The air felt chilled and the thermometer on the shelf read: 32 degrees. The orange juice remained half-frozen. It should still be fresh—he had carefully inspected the date while buying the Minute Maid last night at the Wawa.

Carl turned the thermostat even lower.

The spuds seemed fine. Rawlings cut out any eyes or spots suspected of corruption. Maybe it was the butter. The slab of butterfat slanting off the top of the mashed taters looked horrible. He gagged imagining the rancid paddy sliding down his gullet, first bumping on the dinky do-thing hanging in his throat. Disgusted, Carl vomited all over his meal.

"Mon Dieu!" he lamented. "Why can't I eat anything?"

Standing tempestuously, Rawlings tilted the edge of the Formica and tipped the table forward. The chair fell backwards as pulped potatoes slid earthward.

In a whirl, the hypochondriac attacked the kitchen, opening cabinets and hurling dishes onto the floor.

As Carl sprawled in the aftermath, the neon word NITROGEN blinked crazily in his brain. "Don't they pack those freakin' Oscar Mayer cold cuts in nitrogen?" he wondered.

Rawlings recollected his high school chemistry class and recalled that oxygen could be stripped out of the air using tiny capillary tubing, leaving pure nitrogen.

"No air, no rot, no spoilage!" he gurgled happily.

A workmate helped haul the five hundred pound tank up the stairway. As they sucked on Papst Blue Ribbon (beer in sealed bottles tasted okay to Carl) his buddy asked what the liquid nitrogen was for.

"Nothing special, Alex," Carl lied, staring directly into his friend's eyes. "This evening, I'm cooking a batch of crank in my bathroom and use the gas to form mondo crystals."

"Sounds copasetic to me," Alex said, shaking hands. "See ya later pal."

As soon as Alex left, the electrician began the preparations. Painstakingly, he caulked every nook and cranny in the kitchen. Three hours and twenty-seven tubes of silicone later, the room was hermitically sealed.

Rawlings opened the valve and the frigid gas filled the chamber.

"Nitrogen," obsessive Carl gasped, before passing away.

Barfly *(Act I)*

BARFLY LAY IN BED, his eyes bulging as the whole house shook like a True Value paint shaker. The evening had begun quietly, the usual bar hop imbibing drink after drink until he was so pissed, he couldn't see straight. Booze did not cost Barfly a cent—the dipsomaniac swiped half-full bottles and glasses while their owners were disco dancing or snorting coke in the restrooms.

Leaving the club long after midnight, the inebriate looked for a place to flop, winding up in an upper middle class neighborhood in Hackensack, New Jersey. Barfly's modus operandi was to find a residence with no one home, break in, and crawl into a nice cozy bed. In the afternoon he would awake and raid the liquor cabinet.

This morning, the drunkard made a colossal mistake. Barfly had broken into the House of Satan.

Lara Meets Timothy

THE TRIP TO THE HOSPITAL was disconcerting for Lara. Daylight flashed across the girl's pale face. The glare of the bus windows amplified the stroboscopic effect the bare branches made rushing before the sun. Her forehead ached as she reclined in the seat.

"Do you want a cigarette?" Joan asked, holding out a crushed pack of Marlboros.

Turning to her best friend, Lara shook her head. "Nah, my stomach is all messed up. I really don't think this is such a good idea," she exhaled.

"It's okay. Today will be fine," Joan comforted, smoky breath clouding Lara's face. "Perhaps, the hospital is not as dreadful as they say, but I got to tell you, I'm sort of nervous too."

"Oh, I don't know what I'm doing here," Lara blurted, her cheeks reddening. "I realize that he's my cousin and I get that he asked for me to come. Timothy's dying, but my God, why me?"

The coach shuddered careening down the ramp at the Bartonville, Illinois exit. Nestled between pines, a white church steeple rose in the distance.

The letter had arrived two days ago. Lara found the envelope with the scrawled writing on her bed when she came home from school. It read:

Dear Cousin Lara,

I guess it has been a while since you've heard from me. I've been sick, but you presumably already know that. They won't say what's wrong with me. Sometimes, I wish I wouldn't wake up. Please come visit me. There's nobody else I can turn to. Remember to bring the efink.

Love,

Your Cousin Timothy

Lara lay face down on the patchwork bedspread for a while before showing the letter to her mother.

Her mom thoughtfully sighed and studied her firstborn. "I don't understand what this 'efink,' means. Maybe it's a mistake. If you go up there Lara, be prepared. Timothy's not been himself for a while—he's in a mental hospital. Even Aunt Susan won't go visit. My sister can't bear to see her son locked up."

Lara, more confused than ever, cried herself to sleep that night. It was more than she could take.

The bus glided through the empty streets of Bartonville—only minutes away now. Lara's heart fluttered, her mind concocting excuses to turn around.

"Lara, we get off here," Joan said, nudging with her elbow. "Come on, let's go."

Signaling the driver to stop, the girls descended onto the windswept corner. An iron gate led to Warren's Home for the Severely Disturbed and Handicapped. The building was massive, a tall brick structure featuring solid windows made of glass block. Even so, the woeful screaming filtered to the street. Although it was a little after four o'clock, the sky darkened—a forlorn prelude to winter.

"Pretty creepy," Joan whispered as steamy nicotine billowed from her flared nostrils. The coach accelerated away, a poster of a curvy bikini-clad woman slugging a Papst Blue Ribbon plastered to the side. One of the raggedy crows hopping about, pecked at its amputated leg.

"Well, let's go see crazy Timmy," Lara spoke into the swirling leaves. "We can find out why his mother won't come here."

Bracing against the chill, the pair climbed the steps of the institution. Once safely inside, they approached the coffee-sipping matron manning the main desk. A uniformed guard leaning against the wall tilted his cap.

"We're here for Timothy Dutton," Lara stuttered. Gall rose in her throat, bitter sour. She wished for a glass of water and a handful of Rolaids.

"Timothy Dutton? Yes, that's right. We have a Timothy Dutton. Is he your brother?" the receptionist questioned, lips wet with caffeine.

"No. He's my cousin. I mean, he's my aunt's son. No, he's not my brother," Lara finished, face beet-red.

"She's not his sister, okay?" Joan confirmed, getting a mite riled.

"Sorry, I was just asking, that's all," the woman muttered, pushing several documents forward. "Please fill these out completely and honestly."

Lara and Joan sat on the vinyl couch beside the magazine rack, using a clip-board to write. The forms were confusing and complicated: the questions extremely personal and direct.

"They're asking me if I 'have any fetishes.' Can you believe this?" Lara asked her friend. "This is bullshit! Who cares what brand of tampon I use?"

"Fill them out. Write down Super Plus Tampax and that you love smelly feet. It is purely a formality. Let's drop by your cousin and get the hell out of here. This place is fucked up." Joan pushed several fingers under her nose. "And it reeks in here too."

Applications completed, Lara handed the pages to the receptionist. Without a cursory glance, she scribbled out visitor passes. "Stop by Julius over there. He'll get you prepared."

The guard led them to an alcove. "You're gonna have to put these on," Julius said, indicating a rack of purple gowns. "Leave your clothes and personal items on that table. They'll be safe. Since we're only going to the East Ward, you don't need to be strip searched. Please look at these instructions and I'll be back shortly." Their escort left them to change.

"Read this thing, Lara. This is a fucking nuthouse!" Joan cussed as she undressed. "It says we should wear goggles to avoid getting gassed."

"What?" Lara responded. She struggled with the flimsy gown, trying to determine which side was the front.

"Dude, the patients throw shit and piss cocktails on you," Joan groaned, pulling neoprene-coated gloves up her forearms.

Their chaperone returned several minutes later. "Let's go ladies. Visiting hours end in a thirty minutes."

The girls followed Julius along a hallway to another guard station. A sentry wielding a club verified their papers and swung open the last gate.

"This is it, miss. Have you ever been to visit him?" Julius questioned, stopping at a metal door with a circular peephole.

Lara, not noticing his concerned stare, answered, "No. Why?"

"Timothy Dutton has a very unusual affliction. The patient is strapped to a hospital bed and is in extreme pain, even with the elevated doses of medications he is taking. Mr. Dutton isn't violent to others, but the doctors think he wants to hurt himself."

The guard keyed the lock and stepped aside. The edges of the chamber were dark, a spotlight illuminating the massive object on the bed. Lara squinted in disbelief. The thing on the mattress was humanoid. Not a normal person, no sir, no ma'am. It was a man with an enormous head. Gigantic might be a better word to describe the bloated orb.

In unison, the girls inhaled, emitting earth-shattering shrieks. Lara's hands raked her face, scratching horrible stripes. Joan's fingers shoved deep in her mouth stifled a geyser of vomit. The cloying stench went unnoticed as the friends raced in tight circles.

The ginormous head sluggishly rotated toward the visitors, basketball-sized eyes beckoning pity. A dark fluid flowed from the thick hoses exiting his proboscis.

"The knife, Lara. The knife. Did you bring the knife?" Timothy Dutton's mammoth mouth inquired.

Astronaut

NEIL SAT IN A SMALL Pepto Bismol-tinted hospital room fiddling with a faded Rubik's Cube. Mimicking a scratched record, the man repeated homemade rosary prayers under his breath. An orderly entered and tilting Neil's head—in went a jumble of pharmaceuticals.

"You know, I've been to the moon," the patient mumbled, his fingers walking across the table.

"Right you are, Admiral," the caregiver agreed.

When the nurse left, Neil involved himself again with the multicolored toy.

"I'll get this yet!" the spaceman chuckled, foam flecking the corners of his inverted grin.

Old Men Chatting

DEVOURING AN EGG MCMUFFIN at McDonalds, I observed the three senior citizens. The chaps wore plaid shorts, golfing shirts, hush puppies and caps. This must be their breakfast hangout.

"Yeah, yeah, yeah, you've got to have your cholesterol checked every year," the elderly gent with the swollen abdomen recommended. "My triglycerides are off the chart."

"Well, I took a long trip yesterday and after getting home, I went right to bed and slept until seven this morning. Thank God for that," the tired man with the crooked spine and dyed black hair whined. "And I even managed to eat this greasy sausage without my acid reflex kicking in. Praise the Lord for infinitesimal miracles. I'll see you," he groaned, getting to his feet.

Outside, the hunchback passed by the window gripping a newspaper under an arm. Inky java spilled as he tripped on a crack. The retiree's lips spread in a shit-eating grin as he nodded animatedly to his laughing cronies.

Leaning in, I struggled to catch the remaining conversation, wondering if they might badmouth the cripple now that he had departed. I would overhear no mockery from these old-timers.

"—want to stop breathing," Swollen Abdomen said.

"Well, you can stop breathing anytime," the fellow with the cigarette voice advised.

Swollen Abdomen said something unintelligible.

"Stop. Quit inhaling. No one says you have to breathe," Cigarette Breath urged.

"No, no. I just can't stop. That's not what I want to do," Swollen Abdomen mumbled.

"Hell yeah, pull a plastic bag over your head. That will stop you!" Cigarette Breath chuckled.

"Hmmm, I don't want to die in bed, that's for sure," the geriatric with the inflated belly laughed, wiping hash browns from his grey mustache.

Strange Baby

EFRAIN HENDERSON UNDERSTOOD something was terribly wrong. That is why he immediately made an appointment with a recommended pediatrician.

Sebastian was born a healthy baby, or so that is what Mr. and Mrs. Henderson had been told at the hospital nursery. Sure, his son had all his fingers, eyes and toes, but he additionally came equipped with several otherworldly attachments.

"Come on now, Doc," Mr. Henderson choked, almost swallowing the words in panic. "How could my Sebastian become this, this—?"

"Efrain, it is not very common, but genetic abnormalities are not as rare as they were before we started ingesting so many artificial additives."

Mrs. Henderson lay sideways on the living room couch, gently banging her permanent wave against the armrest. "What are we going to do now, Efrain?"

Efrain restrained himself by only kicking the television stand. "How the hell am I supposed to know? What do I look like, a freakin' rocket scientist?" With that outburst, he hurled the *TV Guide* fall pre-view issue at his wife. "It's entirely your fault anyways, Gladys. You're always eating those goddamn Fiddle Faddles."

The couple lay separated by grief and hostility in their frilly four-poster bed. Efrain abruptly sprung upright, sweat beading his brow and dark eyes whirling. "I am planning to kill Sebastian. And Gladys, you're going to help!"

The Bulb Changer

KENT YACKEE ROLLED OVER ONCE AGAIN. Four sleepless hours had passed since he crawled into bed. "One hundred twenty minutes to go," the handyman whispered, focusing on the alarm clock.

Yackee was very nervous, for today would be the day that transformed his life.

Kent thought he had a shitty job at the gigantic paper mill. As Head Light Bulb Changer, the handyman's main responsibility was replacing any burned-out fluorescent tubes and informing the union electrician of any faulty fixtures. Not always as easy as it sounds—thousands of lights illuminated the ancient plant and many of the ceilings soared fifty feet high. Several were accessible by catwalks or scaffolds, but most had to be reached with long, rickety stepladders. A rare week passed without Yackee falling and hurting himself.

Originally, Kent had been ecstatic to land the job. Kazakhstan was his mother country. The boy grew up in a cement tenement teeming with riffraff and refugees. At sixteen, he landed a gig on an oil tanker as a cook's apprentice. Yackee absorbed the salty abuse for six months. On shore leave in New York City, the adolescent had simply not returned to the ship.

In Jersey City, the immigrant stayed with eight relatives living in a small studio apartment. Kent had higher hopes than this. Kent was ambitious.

"How can I get greenbacks? Fat stacks?" he asked Uncle Zephle.

"This is the United States!" the wizened guru stated. "You can do or be anyone you want. This is the land of the free and the home of the brave. God bless America!" The old man continued singing the "Star Spangled Banner," as Yackee left the room.

Kent felt obligated to pay rent, so he filled out an application at the mill. Milo, his boss, was a hard man and a strict disciplinarian.

"Get those bulbs put away, idiot!" the fat man yelled. "Then check the fixtures on level seven."

"I need to reach my potential," the illegal alien grumbled. "Yackee has a brain and must use it."

Utilizing the electrical skills learned watching purloined VHS cassette tapes, Kent experimented with light bulb modification. He wanted a fluorescent fixture that would explode, sending razor-sharp bits of glass through the air. The problem was getting all the lights to detonate at once. Inserting Radio Shack electronic parts into the ballasts of the tubes, Yackee could fire the bombs using a remote control garage door opener.

July eighth went down as the day Kent Yackee changed history. During the previous three months, he had replaced twelve hundred light fixtures in the factory with altered components. Enormously aroused, the handyman killed twenty-nine of his co-workers.

Jackie the Hun

Jackie always wanted to be a cop.
He wanted to have a big gun.
Just like his brother, his sister, his pop.
Oh, what a way to have fun!
Jackie shot his way to the top.
And marched his way into the sun.
The killing, the killing never stopped.
They called him Jackie the Hun.

Mort's List

MORT CHALUPA EASED BACK in the seat and threw his feet up on the desk. Upon his lap, the latest issue of the *Exquisite Corpse* lay open at the centerfold. The funeral director smirked at the glossy images of "Embalming Botch Jobs."

One photograph depicted a customer on display completely preserved, virtually lifelike. The other picture was of a young man in a mahogany coffin, his features as withered as the flowers Mort regularly discarded behind the Chalupa Funeral Home each night.

"Jeez, what a mess," he muttered, tossing the magazine into the trash. Chalupa shifted in the chair, pulling himself closer to write. Smiling, the orderly man created a list:

1. Check the ventilation in the Spring Room.
2. Purchase more air fresheners.
3. Feed the cat - you remember what happened last time!!!
4. Drain Mr. Aberwacky.
5. Box-Up Miss Stevens.
6. Cut fingernails (mine).
7. Take Mom for a ride.

Mort had a full plate, so he got started pronto. The Spring Room was at the end of the hallway. Papa had appropriately named the chamber because of the eastern exposure. The morning sun filtering through the mauve drapes always created a cheerful atmosphere.

The mortician pulled a footstool from the closet and placed it under the exhaust vent. Located directly above the casket, the carefully designed narrow opening inhaled unpleasant odors. Chalupa held a hand up to the vacuum and did not feel any suction. "No wonder it stinks in here," he grouched.

Hopping down, Mort went to the basement. The cellar was full of discarded funeral parlor bric-a-brac. Pulling in his stomach to squeeze past an antiquated lead-lined embalming table, he investigated the air conditioning unit. The fan was spinning, so Chalupa returned upstairs. Continuing the troubleshooting, he snagged a Mass memorial card from the waste bin and held it across the slit. The paper wasn't pulled upwards.

"Christ," Mort groaned, setting to work with the screwdriver tip of his Leatherman multi-tool. Awkwardly leaning forward, he loosened the fasteners, careful not to drop the cover. A stuck screw required force. The vent cover dropped, spilling dirt, hair and mummified flies onto Judy Stevens' face. Likewise known as "Motorcycle Mama," Judy had once been a very pretty, very pregnant teen until she fell off her old man's chopper.

"Goddammit!" the mortician blasphemed, disturbing the quiet solitude. He leapt to the floor eyeing the enormous hairball on Judy's mouth. About to blow the debris away, he stopped and realized that no one else would see Judy Stevens again, *not ever*. Chalupa slammed the coffin lid before screwing the exhaust vent cover back on. The funeral director crossed 1 and 5 off the list.

An especially glorious fall day, so Mort decided to pick up air fresheners. Priding himself on efficiency, he first initiated the embalming procedure on Fred Aberwacky. As the undertaker jammed a lengthy intravenous needle into the elderly man's arm, the congealed, dark blood trickled into the drain.

Fester, the mortuary's mascot and chief mouse-eater waited impatiently by the door. As Mort edged by, the cat purred and rubbed against his leg.

"Hold on, girl. I'll go get you something to eat." Grinning, he gave the perky feline a quick scratch.

Mort grabbed his leather jacket and headed to the A&P supermarket in nearby Deposit, NY. Glade Hawaiian Breeze was on sale, so he threw four cases into the cart. The undertaker only bought one can of cat food. He needed Fester to be hungry since the Manx made a better rodent-hunter when she was starving.

At the funeral parlor, Chalupa made his weekly rounds replacing the air fresheners. There were twenty in each room hidden under couches and inside silk plants. This backbreaking job finished, the mortician went to check on Fred Aberwacky.

"Get off, get down!" Mort yelled at Fester, who greedily fed upon the cadaver's abdomen. The sneaky cat sprang off the table and meowed. "Bad kitty! Such a naughty girl." Shaking his head, he pulled the needle out of the dead man's arm and checked-off numbers: 2, 3, and 4 from the list.

Fingernail clippings fell to the Oriental rug as Mort called into the Spring Room. "Hey Mom, pack your things. It's time to go for a ride to the cemetery!"

Barfly *(Act II)*

BARFLY BOUNCED LIKE POPPING CORN on Satan's bed. The portal shot open and the Devil himself marched into the master suite.

"What the Hell are you doing in my bed?" Lucifer asked, his tongue shooting kaleidoscopic flames.

"Just trying to catch a couple Z's," Barfly blubbered.

"Boy, I'll make you a fair proposition," the one-eyed goat said to the drunkard. "I'll take your soul in exchange for a lifetime supply of Heineken."

"Heineken? I want Papst Blue Ribbon!" Barfly demanded.

New Face

MATHEW BARRINGS' HAND SHOOK as he signed the papers and passed the check over the desk.

"This is your first payment, Mr. Barrings," the thin-lipped clerk specified, stamping the check. "There will be eleven more. Please step this way and an attendant will show you to your quarters."

Head hanging, Mathew followed the green-gowned, shapeless nurse into the west wing of Saint Vincent Hospital. "Gorgeous day, isn't it? I'm taking Allison and Katy, my children, to the park tonight," she prattled. "They're. . ."

Ignoring the woman's blather, Mathew brooded over the events leading to his admittance into the hospital. It started as a drunken prank. On the drive home to New Jersey from a Duran Duran concert at Madison Square Garden with his buddies, Mathew had jerked the wheel out of Mark's hands, sending the automobile into the opposite lane. Mark and his other friends, Luke and John, were killed outright after the car flipped and hit the Atlantic City bound coach. Twelve people on the bus had been injured, everyone currently filing lawsuits.

Barrings escaped death by flying through the window. The metal, glass and asphalt scraped much of the flesh from his skull, leaving him utterly faceless.

Three days later, he had awoken to the sound of screaming. At first Mathew thought it was somebody else, but eventually realized that he was the one ululating.

"It's okay son," the kindly emergency room intern whispered to his whimpering patient. "You've been through a life-changing ordeal, but as you can be pleased to note; you've survived! How about a nice bowl of strawberry ice cream?"

Mathew had drifted in and out of unconsciousness for several weeks, lethargically returning to reality. Arms and legs strapped tight, a medic securely taped his face with surgical gauze. The moment finally came when his new visage was ready to be revealed. Barrings smashed the hand mirror. *I am a monster.*

Snapped into reality, Mathew heard the registered nurse say, "Right in here, sir. I think you'll be very comfortable. Doctor Osterholm will be along shortly. Put your feet up and try to relax."

Alone in the frigid chamber, Mathew curled into the fetal position and cried.

Later that afternoon, Doctor Osterholm dropped by. "I'm glad you made yourself at home, Mr. Barrings. Please come over here," the plastic surgeon coaxed, indicating the circular table by the window. "We have important issues to discuss."

Mathew reluctantly joined the doctor. Rows of charts and photographs lined the table.

The doctor pushed the stethoscope's bell into the pocket of his white lab coat. "As a matter of fact, you're very lucky. Believe it or not, it is easier to mold a whole new face than to try to reconstruct the original. The slate's wiped clean, so to speak."

"But Doctor Osterholm, I liked my old face," Mathew sighed, studying the before and after portraits of successful and not so successful patients in the picture album.

"Yes, I'm sure you did, my boy. But you realize, it's just the way things are, nothing remains the same. And honestly, you can't walk around like that. I am going to ask you several questions. We should be able to come up with something perfectly adequate. I'm confident you'll love the future you, so let's be positive and give it a try."

Barrings nodded dully.

"Fundamentally, do you desire to be a man or woman? Ha! Ha! I'm kidding. I always say that to my patients. Humor lightens things up, don't you agree?"

A tear welled in Mathew's lidless eye.

"Do you have any preferences as to your appearance? Meaning, are there any movie stars or celebrities that you always desired to impersonate?" the doctor asked, thumbing through a well-paged *People* periodical. "Our team can make you resemble anyone, living or dead."

Mathew scratched his fingers across the molten landscape that was his face. Rolling his eyes, Barrings murmured, "Can you make me into—" Falling silent, his chapped lips attempted to cover chipped teeth.

"That's okay, son. Give it careful consideration. We can decide in the morning. I'll leave you with a few magazines to browse through." Coattails flapping, Doctor Osterholm rushed from the room.

Nine days later, a figure resembling a purple Howdy Doody was seen wheeling away from Saint Vincent Hospital.

Fatherhood

AMOS CHANCE SAT ON HIS FRONT PORCH surveying the scenery. He saw an ugly landscape. A variety of cars and trucks rushed by within inches of the stoop—twenty-four hour traffic, every day of the week. Amos' father told him that his grandpa bought the property years before the state completed the highway. Harry Chance was a deadbeat dad and a liar. Amos knew that his deceased old man had won this beat-up catchall for cigarette butts and beer cans in a card game. Rush hour drove him berserk.

Chance scowled at each car that drove past. He hated all the drivers, especially the ones that looked at him. God, how he loathed being on display. Speeding by, the bastards deliberately turned their heads to evaluate him.

The icy beer felt nice running laughingly down his parched throat. Amos drained the brown bottle and tossed the dead soldier over the guard rail onto the road. A semi-trailer truck advertising "Jesus Christ Is Lord - *Not A Swear Word*" shattered the glass.

Inside the exhaust-blackened house, a miserable baby cried, its tiny eyes riveted to the corner of the room as if seeing a gargantuan spider. This was Amos' offspring, or so he imagined. Last night, Chance had discovered the newborn in a milk crate on his doorstep. A note pinned to the child's chest labeled Amos as the procreator.

Amos had taken the box into the kitchen and gaped at the strange contents before bringing the little guy upstairs into the guest room. There were never any visitors at the "Route 3 Road House" as Harry liked to call their 1950s prefab.

In the wee hours, Amos named the stubby boy Andy and gave the infant a few slurps of beer prior to leaving for work. He worked at the Good Year Service Center in Paramus, New Jersey, slapping tires onto vehicles with thin rubber. As Chance jacked up a Chevrolet Monte Carlo, he knew God had given him a mission. Amos was going to be the best father the world had ever seen. On the way home he picked up a Swanson Hungry-Man TV dinner for himself and two jars of pureed carrots for the kid.

"Andy, Daddy's home!" Amos bellowed, entering the foyer.

"Blub, blub, blub," the baby replied and started squealing.

"Shush, shush, shush," Amos cooed. "I'm gonna buy you a mocking bird," the tire-changer sang to the starving boy.

This routine continued up till the evening Amos got pissed. As usual, he sat on the porch giving motorists the evil eye. A hub cap spun off an old jalopy and ricocheted off the garbage cans. The racket woke up Andy.

"You bastard!" Amos hissed through clenched teeth. Incensed, he scooped up the metal and hurled the disk at a speeding BMW. Passenger side window open, the spinning Frisbee pegged the female driver in the neck, causing a fatal pileup.

The police hauled the belligerent Amos Chance away. Protective of his son, he kept the baby's whereabouts a secret for weeks.

Princess

PRINCESS LAY DROOLING, her snout pressed up against the dishwasher. After eating a watery bowl of Gravy Train, her stomach churned, uncomfortably bloated. Although the canine felt ready to blow chow, she was happy—for Princess lived a dog's life.

Princess was a born a poodle—a super intelligent poodle, mind you. Not one of those stupid mongrels that you observe sniffing around trees and whatnot, but a purebred French Poodle, although she had never been out of Camden, New Jersey. Oh, and I also must mention that yes, the tail-wagger sported an idiotic Poodle haircut. As I said earlier, the hound was smart. Princess could roll over, shake hands and rarely moved her bowels on the shag carpet inside the plush condo that she considered home.

The people that had saved her from Bowwows, the local shopping mall's puppy mill, were very nice. Keenan worked as a financial consultant and Alice kept busy as an interior designer. The couple remained pleasant until Keenan lost his job.

"Holy Mary, Mother of God!" Alice screamed at her melancholic husband. "What were you thinking?" She was livid.

"I'm sorry," Keenan mourned into the tumbler of bourbon. "You know I'm skilled and it won't take long to get another job. Don't you agree?"

"You're a stupid idiot. I just got my new Chrysler LeBaron. How are you going to pay the lease now?"

Princess sensed *The Man's* distress. Stretching, she rose to her manicured feet and went to *The Man's* side, rubbing her massive hairdo against his thigh. For you see, Princess was an affectionate and thoughtful doggy.

Alice raged in full force. Her sharp features hardened as she spat bullets. "You need to talk with Mr. Benton and get your job back. Tell him you're sorry for screwing up. Say anything, but you've got to return to work!"

"Okay, Alice. Please leave me alone." Keenan poured three fingers of Jim Beam.

"Leave you alone? You're the asshole that lost his job, not me!" Gesturing wildly, Alice's vermouth dotted the couch.

Princess squinted her warm brown eyes at all the commotion. As I cited, Princess was a clever pet, but not canny enough to understand the gist of the conversation. The beast had the aptitude to realize she was about to be kicked in the side by *The Woman*. Man's best friends aren't always that great at getting out of the way and she took the full blow. Two ribs splintered as Princess howled in pain.

"Princess, Princess!" Keenan sobbed.

"There. I hate you *and* your stupid bitch!" Alice blared, ready to strike again.

Keenan cradled Princess. The dog labored to breathe and flecks of blood streaked his cheek as she slobbered. Gosh, how he loved that nutty pooch.

Alice grabbed Princess from her husband's arms. The spacious condo had a laundry room. His wife threw the animal into the dryer and turned the knob to cotton. In agony, Keenan muffled his ears as Princess spun, her yelping muffled.

"How do you like that, sport?" Alice cajoled, kicking at the machine. "This mutt's history!"

Keenan, a sensitive man, fell to his knees in hysterics. "Oh, my little baby," he bawled.

Alice opened the Kenmore and hauled out the smoking dog. Princess was very fluffy and had difficulty walking straight.

Dragging Princess by her puffy tail, she marched to the kitchen. "Bye-bye, fleabag," the interior designer sputtered, as she made an effort to jam the poodle's head down the garbage disposal. The poofy coiffure would not fit in the drain. "You're gonna pay," the woman murmured, pressing buttons on the microwave.

Keenan plunged the sharpest chef's knife he could find into his demented wife's bosom.

Later that night, as Keenan cuddled alongside Princess in their big king-sized bed, the pair dreamed of driving fast with the windows rolled down and endlessly chasing sticks.

Abuse

ALBERT ABERWACKY COULDN'T UNDERSTAND why everyone was so upset. *Holy moly, it was only a Class A misdemeanor!* His wife, his family and friends now shunned him. They came up with the bail, but after that, nobody wanted anything to do with the twenty-four-year-old corpse abuser.

His dad died on Tuesday evening after bowling three mediocre games at the Deposit Lanes. Fred Aberwacky, pleased with his final score had seated himself at the alley bar to hoist a few before walking to his empty apartment. Doris, his life mate, passed away eleven months ago, leaving a dark and dreary shell of a home. Fred usually needed a few drinks and an Ambien to fall asleep.

Aberwacky was halfway through his third Papst Blue Ribbon when a teammate thumped him on the back with a meaty braced hand.

"Well done, Big Guy," Chumpy praised, striking Fred square in the middle of his *"No Deposit-No Return!"* team T-shirt.

The beer nuts went down the wrong pipe, followed by a colossal choking fit. This really set Chumpy to whacking Fred's spine. The third smack was the impact that sent the tiny clot of fat on its meandering trip to the doomed bowler's brain. Later in the emergency room, the doctor penciled in "Cerebral Vascular Attack" on the death certificate.

Albert went crazy when he got the news. He had been close to the old guy after his mother died. Fred mellowed out substantially in his golden years. The days of the belt and backhanded slaps were essentially forgotten by both. His dad was now content with his stress-free lifestyle.

June made all the funeral arrangements with Mr. Chalupa. Albert's sister was handy with that type of thing. The wake was scheduled for Saturday morning, at ten o'clock.

The somberly-dressed family gathered in the hallway of the Chalupa Funeral Parlor, a stately ninety-year-old establishment. Multiple generations of undertakers had lived, worked, and died (embalmed by their sons) in the timeless decor of the Victorian home. Nobody cried yet, but everyone was on edge.

Unhurriedly, the mourners filed into the sunny Spring Room. Fred Aberwacky lay stretched out in his favorite plaid suit. To family and guests, Fred appeared cadaverous.

Albert arrived stewed on flavored fortified wine.

"Your father looks marvelous," Mrs. Tarkenton complimented, a sympathetic smile etched upon her wrinkled face. "Mr. Chalupa did a real nice job, don't you think?"

"Yes he did. My pop seems thinner," Albert replied, handling the bottle of Night Train Express stashed in his coat pocket. It was the last of the three he had purchased on the way over.

A hand touched his shoulder. It was Chumpy.

"Son, I'm so sorry," the fat bowler blubbered. "I didn't mean to, you know. Really, I just wanted to—"

"It's okay—not your fault. You were his friend, Chump."

Albert whirled. "Everyone, may I please have your attention. I'd like to say a few words. You were my father's friends. Fred Aberwacky was a fine man, the best, and he died doing what he loved. How many can say that? Now Pop is scoring three hundreds in that great bowling alley in the sky!"

With that eulogy, the remaining Aberwacky pulled the bum wine out of his pocket. In a heady toast, he held the bottle aloft. "This one's for you, Pop!"

The casket crashed to the carpet as Albert drunkenly hauled his father's body from the satin upholstery. The room hushed as he dragged the cadaver by the armpits and set him in an armchair.

"You should be sitting here in the front row, not in that horrible box." Albert pried open Fred's hand and gripped the fingers around the glass. "Drink up. Let's party!" he shouted. Shaking out a cigarette, the son lit the tip before sticking the butt between the sewn-up lips. "Hey ho, the gang's all here," the inebriate sang, surprisingly in tune. "Pop, join in. Everybody please form a conga line!"

The group of mourners gawked silently as Albert Aberwacky made a complete ass of himself. After a few uneasy minutes, the pallbearers dragged Fred's sloshed son out the rear of the funeral parlor and dumped him in a pile of wilted carnations.

Jack Sees Himself

JACK FELT SEXY TONIGHT. All dressed up and nowhere to go, the silver and gold, sequined cocktail dress glistened in the autumn twilight.

"I'd sure like to get some poom poom," Jack whispered to the pecking chickens.

A cow wailed painfully, returning him to the stark reality of his bitter life.

"I'm just a farmer," Jack stated. "A plowboy, a clodhopper, a goddamn weed eater!" Depressed, he kicked at a buzzing pile of sheep pellets.

Jack stomped to the dilapidated farmhouse that was home. Stiletto heels clicking along the slate path, he slammed through the screen door and into the florescent kitchen. On the worn linoleum, the muscular sharecropper gyrated to the Technetronic beat of "Pump up the Jam."

Jack moaned, glimpsing his reflection in the hallway mirror.

"I am a man!" he cried, scaring Trampy off the cat perch. "I am a man! By God, Jack is a man!" the farmer bawled into the now inevitable darkness.

Gym Slut

SALLY WATCHED HER BRONZED REFLECTION glide gracefully along the wall of mirrors. All morning, the *Baywatch* stunt double had pumped iron and messed about with the psyches of the muscular men working out at the local Gold's Gym.

"Hi Silas," Sally greeted a barbarian-sized man adding kilograms to a barbell.

"Duh, hi Sally. How ya doing?" Silas stuttered, his eyes hanging out of his head.

The woman left the halfwit and strutted across the aerobics mats, catching another glimpse of her toned physique on a polished column. The Super-Spa was Sally's crib. Her playthings were men—specifically barbaric Conans with Lilliputian brains and animal instincts.

Sally draped herself over a Nautilus machine. It didn't matter which device, she knew that within minutes a flock of panting musclemen would surround her splendiferous body.

Closing her eyes, Sally pulled on the weight machine's bar. After counting to ten, opening her peepers, she found herself encircled by a dozen or so perspiring male beefcakes. "Hi guys!" the gal cooed as the men rubbernecked.

"We're tired of you teasing us!" Lex, a very short, barrel-chested man hollered. "What do you think we are, just hunks of meat?"

"No," Sally managed to reply; now frightened. "I'm only being friendly, that's all."

"Yeah, right. I know your kind!" Alejandro, a middle-aged Tarzan shouted. "We're gonna teach you a lesson!"

In frenzy, the crowd moved in on Sally. She fought fruitlessly as they grabbed her arms and dragged her off the equipment.

"Gym slut, gym slut!" the he-men chanted.

"We got us a real gym slut here!" Lex established, his face flushed and eyes wild.

The men tossed Sally around the room as if she was a feather pillow, instead of a proper young lady. Flying through the air, the human medicine ball swiftly bruised. The squealing abated as her head dented on the edge of a StairMaster.

Later that evening, as the freshly-groomed bodybuilders sat chatting around the juice bar, their pearly teeth flashed, pumped up from the healthy exercise of the day.

China

SWEAT ROLLED IN RIVULETS from Perry Ellis' grimy brow. The boy was digging a tunnel to China, and it took more time and effort than he originally planned.

Perry had informed his mother of the project after lunch. "Okay honey," she said patting his head. "Dig a hole to China. That sounds like a fine lesson in geography. Don't forget, for dinner we're having your favorite."

His father reluctantly provided the shovel. "Be careful, Son. Don't make a mess," he pleaded before walking away.

Perry chose a place in the northern corner of the backyard. The patch was protected by bushes—the clay soft. He didn't want his friends Miles and Gilberto to see the secret passage. The adventurer figured by suppertime, he'd be gobbling chop suey with Mao Tse-tung.

The digger didn't know it, but he made a poor choice in location. First and foremost, a sump collected sewage directly below his excavation. The cesspool teemed with E. coli.

Secondly, Perry's shaft was flanked by an underground hornet nest to the east and a rattlesnake den to the west. Both species were agitated by the annoying vibrations. Gas lines, electric wires and waterlines intersected several feet beneath the boy.

The spade that Mr. Ellis so thoughtfully provided hit something solid. Using his hands, Perry carefully unearthed a skull and several long skinny bones. They appeared to be human or perhaps simian. Whatever they were, a sizable dent centered the top of the cranium. A welcome find, so the youth put the articles aside for later examination.

The explorer inhaled and dug deeper. Again, he reached an unyielding object. It sounded metallic and by golly, the dark loam revealed a box. The rusty lock gave way, revealing dirty pictures of boys his age and a large plastic penis.

"Neat," Perry said, placing the container next to the funky bones.

Tired of digging, the youngster snacked on M&Ms. If he didn't break through soon, it would be time to quit and go watch television. After all, the summer was long and tomorrow was another day.

Energized with sugar, the child implanted the tip of the garden tool in the soil and pounced onto the blade. Simultaneously, he severed a 440 volt electrical cable and cracked a gas pipe. Perry was electrocuted shortly before his body vaporized in a towering ball of flames.

Later, Mr. Ellis found a stinking pit filled with bloody water. Charred snakes and singed bees floated upon the surface. He hid the dildo in his pocket and went inside for spaghetti and meatballs.

Perry Ellis floated high above the earth. The world was massive and the boy belatedly realized the foolishness of his aspirations.

The Wedding

"WHAT A MAGNIFICENT DAY FOR A WEDDING!" Aunt Shirley proclaimed to the azure summer sky. "June is a lovely month to engage in holy matrimony."

The group of relatives and friends waited by the stairs of Holy Saint of Saints Church, on the outskirts of Bayonne, New Jersey. Karen McPherson (now Mrs. Karen Greenberg) and her husband Walter had completed their marriage rights and happily led the procession away from the altar. The well-wishers pelted the jubilant couple with handfuls of rice and bird seed.

Randall McMullany, a distant relative of Karen, stood beside his mother watching attentively. This was the first nuptials the youngster had ever attended. Randy happened to be stunned by the buxom bride, yet a little apprehensive as well. The white bridal gown blinded his hazel eyes as the twosome dashed toward the rented Rolls Royce. The best man paid an arm and a leg for the limousine and it needed to be returned in an hour.

Randy's mother panned the well-wishers with a Super 8mm camera. These vibrant moments would be recorded on Kodachrome film stock.

As the newlyweds approached, Randy noticed a mark on the bride's dress. Crimson red, a vivid blotch spread like wild fire across the young woman's gown.

"Bloody bride, bloody bride!" Randy chanted, his voice squeaking. "Mommy!" he clamored.

The crowd held their breath as the bride clutched her abdomen, grimacing in horror as she beheld herself.

"Karen!" Walter keened, grabbing his sagging new wife as she pitched headfirst down the church steps.

As the first of the group to reach her daughter, Ann McPherson pulled on Karen's hand, sobbing mightily. "Are you okay, honey?"

"Karen's losing blood fast!" blurted her father, Harry McPherson. "My baby's been shot!"

The crowd hunched, expecting a flurry of high-powered rifle blasts.

"Where is she bleeding?" Matt McRennolds asked. "We have to stem the flow." The young man was an aspiring medical student.

"It's coming from her—" Father O'Reiley gasped.

The guests scatted throughout the church compound, each alone in their own embarrassment.

"Walt, in my bag," Karen whispered to her new husband.

"No way, nope. Uh-I got to get outta here!" Greenberg stuttered as he let his wife's head drop to the consecrated concrete. "This is crazy. You ruined our holy union!" The groom hopped into the waiting Silver Ghost and sped away.

As the sun set on the peninsula of Bayonne, an ancient nun kneeling, scrubbed the stoop of the church. Under her breath, the sister whistled strains of Mendelssohn's "Wedding March."

Edmund Plays Doctor

EDMUND EXAMINED HIMSELF CLOSELY with the stethoscope. Since the doctor had not yet entered the office, the youngster played with the medical instruments as soon as the grumpy nurse exited. The stethoscope was a deluxe model: black neoprene hose with stainless steel fittings.

Sitting on the end of the examination table, the youth placed the cool round diaphragm upon different parts of his body. Of course, he began with the chest area. Gently breathing, Edmund listened to the air hissing in and out of his esophagus. The boy coughed, hearing globs of phlegm flip-flopping within his lungs. Edmund smiled, imagining drowning in his own stringy mucus.

Traveling across the lumpy ribs, he slid the sensor to the point where the beats were the loudest. "Ka-thump, ka-thump," his heart pounded. Edmund listened for irregularities. "Grrrumph!" his stomach pleaded. "I'll feed you later, tummy," he told the boisterous digestive system.

Edmund kept an eye out for the doctor. Unable to detect any movement, the young man continued auscultation. Without a care in the world (for he was simply here for a school physical), the lad roved the bell in circular motions about his torso. The innards buzzed like the Ford Motor Plant.

Edmund worked the slippery stethoscope up his throat. A grinding sound came from behind him. Believing this noise to be the cracking of bones in his neck, the adolescent arched his spine and stretched. Noticing a faint clacking, Edmund's hand roamed into the hairline.

Muffled, but still audible in the earpiece, he caught, *"You're an asshole."*

"What?" Edmund croaked, whipping around to see an empty room.

"You heard me. Eddie, you're an asshole. A fucking asshole, to be exact—a hairy, fuckin' asshole. You phony fuck!"

Edmund dropped the medical device as a sharp pain centered at the base of his skull.

Grabbing a mirror on a nearby table, Edmund tilted the flexible wand attached to the small reflector. The hair on the back of his dome clotted dark with blood.

"Somebody must have bit me," Edmund thought irrationally. "Whoever was saying those nasty things attacked me and then ran out of here."

With one hand, he parted hair, revealing a sizable cyst. Blood and a sticky fluid oozed from the sore.

"Jeez, that sucks," Edmund said softly, jaw slack with worry.

The teenager probed the springy mass. A hard object lay just beneath the surface. Using fingernails, he picked at the lump. *Ow that hurts!* The skin tore, unveiling an inflamed node soaked with fresh cream sauce.

Thinking the wound was an ingrown hair, Edmund used both thumbs to squeeze the mound. When the pain became unbearable he stopped, angling the mirror to survey the results.

"H-E-double-toothpicks!" Edmund screaked, viewing the set of razor-sharp ivories jutting at angles from the wound. Saliva and coagulating blood oozed from the crooked mouth. The chipped shark teeth cut gums as they ground together with incredible force.

"Hey Eddie. You're a loser!" the teratoma with the crappy attitude shrilled as the schoolboy rocketed from the fourteenth floor window.

Jack's Bedroom

GIGGLING, JACK FLOPPED ON HIS BELLY across the queen-sized bed. "Yes, yes, Reed. That's so precious!" squealed the burly cross-dresser. Flipping on his back, Jack stretched the telephone cord. "And he's got a great set of gams too. Well, gotta go. I need to get changed for work."

As the farmer hung up, heaps of women's undergarments toppled off the bed.

"Five more minutes, then I'll get up," Jack informed Trampy. The cat played with a bra strap dangling off the bed.

Within minutes, the man's eyes rolled and jittered—he was dreaming.

Jack found himself on an unfamiliar farmstead. The iron plow he manhandled was yoked to a giant ox. Unsurprisingly, the uncastrated bovine wore a set of woman's Jockeys: red bra and black panties. When the draft animal turned to regard his driver, the beast smiled and winked.

"Giddy-yap, little doggie," Jack sang, his voice small and clipped. The team plowed under the hybrid crop on one of the many acres. Shriveled leaves of the uprooted plants blanketed the furrows. Angry storm clouds brewed on the horizon.

Jack glanced backwards to see a pack of wild hounds in close pursuit.

"Faster, Bitsy!" the sharecropper urged the ox. "We must escape!"

The panties on the bovine vanished as he charged ahead. Enormous gonads banged against the rusty plow.

Grey poodles surrounded the plow team. The leader nodded and led the mob downhill.

A flock of nosey crows jeered at the plower's outfit: Osh-Kosh B'Gosh overalls.

"They're just my work clothes!" Jack barked at the wheeling birds. Decorated with colorful patches, the rolled up denim cuffs exposed fashionable pumps. Under the overall's straps, the tiller wore a frilly camisole, low-cut and revealing. Pink nail polish adorned his fingernails, trimmed short for farm labor

An enormous sinkhole loomed ahead. Excited, Bitsy headed straight for the depression. Jack aimed to steer the creature away, but unable to, dove clear at the last moment. The ox and plow vanished over the brink. The pit exposed a junkyard of cast-off farm equipment and bleached skeletons. Unscathed by the fall, Bitsy snuffled at a pair of crusty boots.

Dismayed at his loss, Jack sobbed.

"Don't fret miss," Farmer Ray said gently, resting a mottled hand upon Jack's shoulder. The agriculturalist's features were indistinguishable in the glaring light. "Have you seen my galoshes?" the silhouetted man asked, his naked feet rooted in the fecund earth.

"I am a man! I am a man!" Jack screamed at the shadow.

Jack awoke trembling, the stink of sweat and manure rank within the bedroom. A muffled choking came from under the bed.

"Trampy!" Jack called, dropping to the bare floor. The cat wreathed—paws and claws raking the mattress's underside. A bra strap hung from his mouth.

"Trampy, you swallowed my brassiere," Jack gasped as he gripped the left cup and pulled. "No, I'll rip his insides out!" the plowman blurted, thinking of the strap wrapped deep in the cat's viscera, the hooks buried in delicate organs.

Trampy's eyes rolled up as his labored breathing stopped. Jack prayed to Jesus as he yanked on the 42b cups. The bra strap strained, seemingly caught in the feline's gullet. With an elastic snap, the obstruction came loose catapulting the stomach's contents: Friskies Ocean Whitefish and Tuna Dinner, hairballs, dental floss, and part of a toy mouse. Splattered with vomit, the farmer grinned anyway. Trampy purred passionately and rubbed a furry cheek on his master's sticky chin.

"I love you Trampy," Jack cooed to the happy-go-lucky cat.

An Interspecies Romance

EDWARD KNEW IT WAS MORALLY WRONG, but he touched them anyway.

The boy rolled out of bed and hopped into his slippers. He was already fully dressed, so it only took a moment to descend the stairway, past his grandmother's room and into the backyard.

The barn loomed eerily in the distance, a monumental testament to his father's livelihood. Crickets chirped in stereo as he followed the ancient pathway through the weeds. On the horizon, the moon reflected another day's glow. Edward saw or heard none of this—he was full of anticipation.

"Ee-i-ee-i-oh," Edward sang, creeping into the barn, the gloom split by smoky beams of light seeping through the gaps in the dilapidated siding. The rays undulated across the youth's face as he entered the corral.

"Hi Flower," Edward cooed.

A gentle mooing acknowledged the teenager's presence.

"How ya doing girl?" Edward asked the cow. The adolescent ran his palms lovingly along the beast's hide. Bits of hay and manure dropped to the earth as he brushed Flower's flank. The teats hung like a bunch of bananas from the bovine's plump udder.

"Damn," Edward breathed, as he bathed the mammary gland with soapy water. Eyes closing dreamily, he traced the ropey milk vein along Flower's udder. Tenderly squeezing two fleshy spouts, the adolescent milked the animal into a pail.

Flower moaned with stupid abandon, eyes rolled up into her forehead, one hoof scraping back and forth on the stall's floor.

"I love you Flower," Edward murmured softly.

Laser Cutter

MATT MCRENNOLDS GROANED cracking his vertebrae. Dead tired from partying, the lab technician had been slicing up stiffs all day with the laser cutter. Some corpses he cross-sectioned longitudinally, others laterally. Dissection wasn't a dreadful job, but it sure did get boring. A wad of solidified brain tissue bounced off the protective shield of his face mask, falling into the *"Coffee Makes Me Poop"* mug.

In a rage, Matt kicked at the latex-filled cadaver. "Goddammit!" he screeched, as bits and pieces of Fred Aberwacky flew about the room.

Swim Club

THE SUMMER IS STIFLING HOT AND MUGGY. Above, the sun is an orange ball and with the glare, I cannot see much. My friends want to go swimming. I have no choice; the munchkins drag me to the lagoon's edge and begin an impromptu diving game. Bodies contort as athletes leap into the blue sea. Everyone is laughing. It is my turn and I am scared. Trying to be funny, I cannonball, but I go too deep beneath the waves.

Drowning in brine, I try to get to the surface; however, oxygen is beyond my fingertips. When I finally breach my mirrored reflection, night has fallen and I am alone floating on the ocean. The water tastes coppery and the swells surrounding me are vermilion. Panicking, I check for bleeding, unable to spot my injury—too dark to find the wound.

I hail a passing cruise ship appropriately christened the Titanic. Overhead, geese fly in spreading V-formations throughout our galaxy, the Milky Way.

Now thirsty and hungry, I must get to land. Dog-paddling, I aim toward lights twinkling on the shore. Below the waves, I observe rows of submerged automobiles, trucks, and buses resting among trees and bushes.

Wary, I check my teeth for looseness. On initial examination they are loose, and then they appear firm. At least that is fixed.

Naked and vulnerable, I try swimming on my back, but molting pelicans land on my stomach. A piece of flotsam is within grasp. The ruptured box says *Tomato* in a foreign language. Enjoying the added buoyancy, I kick toward shore.

"Hi," I say, entering the glowing room. "What happened to you guys?" My friends ignore me, watching the geese in the rafters. The birds dart after phosphorescent lightning bugs.

Chasing the moon, the tides have risen again. The fabric on the couch is dark and wet from splashing water.

Dear Margaret

Dear Margaret,

Since December of 1973, I have weighed over 300 pounds. If my high blood pressure or slightly swollen right aorta don't someday kill me, I will do it myself. I've lived through loneliness, depression and despair. I'm an alcohol/heroin/crack cocaine/benzodiazepine/dark chocolate addict and a twenty-two-year-old, divorced mother of three (different fathers I think) living on welfare. I hate myself enough to sell my body to get money for booze and dope. I have suffered humiliation after humiliation. A big gal like me gets all the sadists and perverts that no other prostitute shall take. I have no respect, no hope, no God, no nothing.

Regards,

Nancy (street walker)

Washington, D.C.

+++

Dear Nancy,

Quit your bitching and stop degrading yourself. Get off your back, join a gym and enroll that fat ass in Alcoholics Anonymous and a drug rehabilitation center.

Best wishes,

Margaret (advice columnist)

Chicago, Illinois

Larry's Inheritance

LARRY FELT RIDICULOUS waddling from the bathroom to the bedroom with his pants draped around his ankles. He was sticky.

"Hello, who is it?" Larry shouted into the mouthpiece.

"This is Norman Finch, your Aunt Mabel's insurance agent. Do you remember when she died last month?"

"Yes, of course I do. She was my favorite aunt," Larry lied.

"Well, Mrs. Papules seems to have left you a sizeable life insurance policy. We need you to come in and sign the papers as soon as possible. Westlake Mutual likes to be on the ball."

"How much?" Larry asked, his voice all a quiver.

"Over ten million dollars. Not too shabby, huh?" Norman declared.

"Fuck me! How did she get so much dough?" Larry cawed, his voice raising and constricting.

"Son, your aunt was in bed with the Devil," the insurance agent warned. "There will be heavy tax penalties on that money. As your agent, I suggest you get a good accountant and start going to daily Mass."

Screw-Up *(Part I)*

"GOD'S TEETH!" MR. PREEN SCREAMED. "What are you stupid, Jason?"

Jason backed away from his father. Mr. Preen could be mean as hell. Once for no reason, he slammed his son's head against a steel support column in the basement.

"Now get over there and do it properly this time!" Enraged, Mr. Preen kicked piles of saw dust across the garage.

For multiple weekends, the father and son team ventured to construct a picnic table. The big yearly family reunion was scheduled for the next weekend. Relatives from near and far brought baskets and coolers of food and alcohol. Mrs. Preen demanded they get a table for the guests to dine upon. A light flickered beneath Mr. Preen's bald lid after he realized the prices of new furniture. He could build one himself and Jason would help. They finally got the lumber cut and were about to assemble the mess. Most of the Rickel Home Center planking came warped or split. A jumble of ruined boards lay in the corner of the untidy garage.

"This time when drilling, hold the tool straight. Watch what you are doing!" Jason's father ordered.

The eleven-year-old manhandled the big Sears Craftsman variable speed reversible drill. Eyeing up the hole, he pulled the trigger. The tool bit dug deep and then seized up in a knot-hole. The wood whirled, smashing against his dad's foot.

"Jesus H. Christ. *Jeeeesus Christ!*" Mr. Preen barked as he danced around the driveway. "My ankle! Shit! You broke my goddamn ankle!"

Jason dropped the power tool and scurried. Separated from the house, the two car garage stored lawn tools and unsold yard sale items. The youth darted amongst the junk, desperately trying to avoid the huge grasping hands.

"I'm gonna get you, you little bastard. You can't hide from Daddy!" Mr. Preen spat.

"Sorry Papa!" Jason blubbered, crawling under an overturned steel wheelbarrow.

There, under the protective dome, Jason found his old G.I. Joe Action Figure speckled with leaves and grass clippings. He grabbed the camouflaged figurine and clutched it to his heaving chest. Jason heard his father hunting for him behind a stack of aluminum siding. Sobbing, he contemplated the Joe. The doll resembled a more masculine version of his dad.

In a fit of childish rage, Jason grabbed the army man by the legs and slammed the toy against the concrete floor.

"Damn you, damn you!" the youngster chanted, pounding the plastic helmeted head again and again. The helmet broke off, skittering out from under the wheelbarrow.

"Got you!" Mr. Preen bayed, finding his son's hiding place.

Jason continued pulverizing the G.I. Joe's cranium against the cement. The pressure molded head exploded, splitting along the main seam. The child jolted as the wheelbarrow rocked from his father falling on top. Regulating his breathing, the small boy waited. Something slithered down his spine causing him to twitch. Jason's forehead bashed against the metal as he wrenched around, discovering chunks of skull and lumps of medulla oblongata.

Visiting Grandma

SALVIDOR TWILL HESITATED on the stairs descending to the kitchen. His mom and dad were whispering. This was very unusual, so Sal listened intently.

"Nobody will ever find out. They'll merely think we put Mom in an out-of-state nursing home," his father assured.

"I don't know, Will." His mother's voice sounded strained as she said guardedly, "It makes economic sense, but—"

On the boob tube, the incessant yammering of Regis Philbin and Kathie Lee Gifford momentarily interrupted.

"If we're gonna do this, *it had better be tonight,*" Mr. Twill urged.

Sal cleared his throat and clumped downstairs. In the kitchen, he sleepily asked for smoked sausage and pancakes.

"Hey pal," his dad greeted with false bravado. The dark circles under his eyes confirmed that his mother-in-law had suffered another episode. At regular intervals, the diseased woman hacked up blood and pieces of lung in enormous coughing fits.

"Morning, Salvidor," his mom mumbled. Tiredly, she tousled his unkempt hair. "How did you sleep?"

"Fine, Mom,' Sal fibbed. He had tossed and turned from dusk to dawn as his grandmother rattled the house with her wretched convulsions.

Gnawing the breakfast sausage, the boy prayed that he would never get old like Grandma.

"Well, I'm off," Mr. Twill sighed, chugging the remainder of his coffee. "I'll see you guys later." Smiling, he kissed his wife, squeezed her buttocks, and patted his son on the head. Sal caught the excited winks his parents sent each other.

Staring out the window in Mr. Price's fourth grade class, Sal wondered what might happen that evening.

The next daybreak, Sal awoke as usual. Making his way along the hall, he noticed that Grandma's door was ajar and her room empty. The bed was stripped and the stained pillows were shoved in a garbage bag.

In the kitchen, Mom and Dad appeared exhausted but upbeat. Sal heard the washing machine cycling in the laundry room.

His father clasped him on the shoulder. "Good morning, Son." Yawning, he asked, "Did you sleep well?"

"Yes," Sal replied, this time honestly. Mrs. Twill fervently scrubbed her hands in the sink with brown soap. "Mom, can I go play at Jerry's after school today?"

"Yes honey, but be home by six. Your father and I are going out for a dinner date. Greg is coming to stay with you."

"Okay Mom," Sal promised, leaving the room.

After sunset, as Greg watched Star Trek reruns in the Twill's den, Sal explored the backyard. He didn't fully distinguish what to search for, but finding the new pile of brush pushed against the fence, he deduced that his grandmother was under it.

During the last several months, Sal became fascinated with death and decay. It started when Jerry had shown him the bird.

One boring Saturday, Sal rode his bicycle to the Mulligan's house. Climbing the fence, he located his friend bending over a small excavation in the garden.

"Hi, Jerry," Sal called cheerfully. The boy flinched, but then smiled craftily.

"Hey, man. Take a look at this," Jerry coaxed, continuing to poke the hole with a stick.

To Sal's amazement, a lifeless blue jay lay in the cavity.

"Jesus, Jerry. What is that?" Sal felt kind of sick as his buddy jabbed at the maggots adorning the feathered creature.

"I'm doing experiments. You know—biology and stuff," Jerry answered proudly. "Check this out." The lad proceeded to dig up a series of holes, each containing birds in different stages of putrefaction.

"Oh man, this is cool!" Sal exclaimed. The child now saw the beauty of the project. "You should tag the legs with the date of death."

For the rest of the summer, the two boys conducted casual decomposition experiments. They searched the roadways and forests for specimens. On several occasions, the pair even came upon large mammals: eight flattened cats and a disemboweled Doberman Pinscher. The dead were interred in Jerry's growing garden cemetery.

In the trees, squirrels chattered and everything was lovely in the rural community of Hale Eddy, New York.

Sal pulled away the branches and put boot to shovel. The soil was sandy and the job went quickly. He had no clue how deep his father had buried Grandma, but was sure that this was the right spot.

The youth recoiled. A cyclopean orange eye glared from the bottom of the pit. Upon further scrutiny, Sal chuckled, realizing it was one of the pumpkin-faced bags that his dad had used last fall to scoop up leaves. Tearing away the plastic, Sal unveiled his ancestor.

"Hi, Grandma," Sal said softly to the swollen face.

"Oh, hello Sal," the youngster imagined the drawn purple lips replying.

"How are you doing, Grandma?" Sal inquired, withdrawing his Scout knife. "I'm so glad to see you. You're looking fabulous—I miss you so much."

"I miss you too, Sal. You're my favorite grandson," Grandma rasped to her only grandson. *"Dear, could you please get this dirt off of my face? Oh, yes. Thank you, kind sir."*

Sal brushed the filth from the bloodless woman's face and initiated his examination. He calculated that his grandmother had been in the earth less than twenty hours. This would account for the favorable condition of the body. The arms were crossed over her heart, proof of his father's extreme love for his mother-in-law. The limbs shifted somewhat when Sal tried to bend them. *Rigor mortis*, he determined. This was a Latin word Sal and Jerry researched in the school library.

"Grandma, are you having trouble breathing?" Pressing the heels of his hands, Sal performed cardiopulmonary resuscitation on the shrunken chest. "Row, row, row your boat gently down the stream," Sal sang, hearing the brittle ribs crack. "Merrily, merrily, merrily, merrily, life is but a scream."

The cadaver's mouth popped open, spewing rubbery phlegm.

"That's better," Sal murmured, inspecting the caved-in sternum. "Your airway is cleared."

Grandma moaned, *"Oh, thank you, dear. I feel so much better, although my chest hurts a teeny-weeny bit."*

The Scout knife contained many blades and tools. Sal utilized all of these in his scientific quest for answers.

"What the—?" Greg breathed.

Sal whirled to find his babysitter gaping in shock and awe.

"What are you doing? *Ughh!*" Greg leaned forward, about to chunder.

"I'm doing research, mostly physiology. Take a peek," Sal replied. The boy pointed out the different regions of his grandmother's anatomy.

"Wow, this is great!" Greg exclaimed. The teenager was thrilled. For the balance of that year, with Jerry's help, the triad conducted extensive decomposition studies. They patrolled the freeways for accident victims and buried the bodies in Sal's backyard. The best part was digging them up again.

Penny the Cow

PENNY MOOED PLAINTIVELY as her master cleaned the waste from the stall. Her udder was full and ached like it was about to burst. Nearly thirty-two hours had elapsed since the bovine had been milked. Swollen, her mammary glands filled to capacity.

"Moo, moo?" she cried to the man in the stained overalls.

"Shut up, Penny!" Farmer John replied. "I ain't got no time for yer foolin'. I got me a pile of chores ter do, so let me get back to my doings."

"Fine," the gentle cow murmured. "I'll just die in here if I don't get milked." She thought longingly of the last day her teats were expressed. Oh, the warm ecstasy of spurting milk into the galvanized milk bucket she referred to as her "party pail."

"Moo-moo? Moo-moo-moo!" Penny bawled in panic. "Mooooo!" The cow dropped to her front knees, tail pointed in the air.

"What in tarnation are ya doing, girl?" Farmer John bellowed as the twelve hundred pound Holstein knocked him over and shattered his hip against the barn siding.

Farmer John lay broken. Both legs twisted at asymmetrical angles and the bones ground marrow when he attempted to shift. "Help me," he sobbed in Penny's furry ear.

The overloaded cow wreathed in agony, her milk vein irritated. She spied her beloved party pail wedged under Farmer John's left arm. "Moo-moo! Mooooo!" With her nose, she pushed the bucket to her master. "I wanna get milked!"

Farmer John drifted into unconsciousness—his internal organs mashed and beyond repair.

Moral to this story: *Keep your cow healthy by milking her several times a day and twice on Sunday.*

Leper

IT IS AN UNCELEBRATED FACT that there are over sixty-five hundred people afflicted with leprosy living in the United States. Approximately a third of the two hundred fifty Hansen's disease cases that arise each year result from unprotected contact with infected armadillos. Lenard "Gooey" Torte found this out the hard way.

Lenard grew up as a normal lad until the lunchtime his hand brushed against a Texan loaded to the gills with the bacterium mycobacterium leprae. The accountant had simply been reaching for the DOWN elevator button. Looking over to smile and perhaps say hello, Torte had been shocked by the rancher's horrible deformity. A pair of glittering black eyes peered between mounds of nodules and macules.

As the doors slid open, Lenard rushed to the men's room and painstakingly washed his hands in itchy panic. The incident forgotten, the young man returned to his routine of work and partying. Life was grand.

Seven months later, Torte's fingers and toes began to lose sensation. He attributed the numbness to lack of exercise and joined a local health spa. Lifting the weights was easy in the beginning, although the number-cruncher did notice that instead of growing stronger and bigger, his muscles seemed to atrophy as his body shrank.

Lenard realized he needed medical help when his reproductive organ became inoperative.

Doctor Woodward examined his new patient, thoughtfully studying the scurfy tracings across the back and down the spine. Suddenly the physician withdrew. "Hansen's disease!" he warned his nurse practitioner.

Betty had already run from the clinic, so Woodward pulled the fire alarm and scrambled alone to the medicine cabinet. Forehead beaded with sweat, the petrified physician injected 200 cc of BCG vaccine into his jugular. Finished self-medicating, he speed-dialed the international number for medical emergencies.

Before the sun set, Lenard Torte was unceremoniously shipped in a special quarantine container to a leprosarium near Hyderabad, India.

Pursuit of the Ancients

AT DAYBREAK, THE THREE ANCIENTS descended upon Romeo Apello's New Mexico residence. Waxen, yellow skin peppered with poppy seed spots glimmered as the four-thousand-year-old visitors tested the brick and slate steps. By midmorning, they moved on to the flaking doorframe, peering at the steel door beyond the screen. For an hour, the extraterrestrials conferred in an unknown dialect.

Cocking an antenna, the tall, gamey one skimmed elongated fingers along the vinyl siding that coated the townhouse.

"Free-lee, tu ba-taton," droned the blind Ancient with the gilled face. Its bulbous head gyrated in counter-clockwise circles.

The fat spaceman, scalp weirdly decorated in the mantle of the Botzu, gestured excitedly and joined the conversation.

Radioactive tentacles probed at random in and about the mailbox and doorbell.

Romeo Miller awoke to the insistent ringing of musical chimes. Rolling across his wife Trudy, the truck driver landed on the maple floor.

"Who the fuck, could that be?" Miller muttered, tripping on the piles of clothes littering the bedroom. Feet dragging and rubbing his eyes, the homo sapien stood at the front door.

"Who is it?" the trucker asked, leaning his forehead against the cool wood.

There was no response, so Miller swung open the only barrier between here and eternity. A war cry of incredible clarity preceded the two beryllium spears that pierced the man's heart and lungs. As Romeo lay exploring true suffering, and death in that order, he wondered who had sent the Ancient hit men, now stepping over him into the condominium.

The Stroke: A Dramatic Performance

Stage: A small platform is appropriate for this Off-Broadway production. A temporary wall or curtain can be utilized to separate the two rooms (living room and kitchenette). The kitchenette contains a counter containing a sink and stove. A window is located above the faucet. The sparse living area is furnished with a well-worn Barcalounger and a black and white console television.

Actors: The characters in this play are not married, but have been living together for two turbulent months.

> The woman: Helen is a voluptuous former model in her mid-thirties.
>
> The man: Eddie is fifty years old and balding. He is part owner of a failing chain of car washes. Eddie convinced Helen to give up her modeling career.

Opening scene: The woman is busy making tuna melts in the kitchenette. The man is viewing professional baseball on the television. It is twilight in their Manhattan condominium.

Helen speaks first: *Honey, could you please take out the trash?*

Eddie: *Uh-huh.*

Five minutes pass. Helen continues working in the kitchenette humming and chopping vegetables. Eddie stares raptly at the television screen. *(Director's Note: Three hundred seconds in a play without speech or stirring activity is an extremely long time to keep the audience attentive. The actress must carry this scene with lively singing or whistling and natural burning sexuality.)*

Helen: *Eddie, what about the garbage?*

Eddie: *Just a minute, dear. I'm watching the game. All the bases are loaded and Strawberry is up to bat.*

Helen sounds irritated: *Is that more important than giving me a hand? I'm in here cooking dinner for you.*

Eddie stands up. Darryl Strawberry hits a towering grand slam over the fence. Eddie sits down pounding a fist into a baseball glove.

Eddie: *What's for supper, babe?*

Helen noisily drops a sauce pan into the kitchen sink.

Helen is now very irritated: *What do you mean, "What's for supper?" You can't even take out the fucking garbage!*

Eddie's voice hardens: *I will. Keep your skirt on. Stop being such a bitch.*

Helen is practically yelling: *Who are you calling a bitch? You're just a stupid car washer. I made more money in an hour on the catwalk than you do in a—*

Eddie's body quakes with rage. He has a short temper and ultra-high LDL cholesterol.

Closing scene: Silence in the condominium, except for the shouts of cheering Mets fans emerging from the television's speaker. The man's face registers agony before slumping lifeless in his precious Barcalounger. In the kitchenette, the woman leans against the sink rubbing her temples and gazing out at the twinkling lights of the evening skyline.

The End

Screw-Up *(Part II)*

JASON WAITED ANXIOUSLY for his mother's approval. Mrs. Preen sniffed before tasting the concoction.

"What is this crap, Jason?" the large-boned woman complained. Her family came from working stock and was notorious for hotheadedness. "I told you to simmer it, not fry it, you stupid moron." Brandishing a wooden spoon, Mrs. Preen chased after the fourteen-year-old.

Jason scampered upstairs to his cluttered bedroom. Pressed against the locked door, he waited.

"Boy, you come out of there. This is your mother. You know you can't hide from Mommy!" Mrs. Preen's breath moistened the Mötley Crüe poster plastered to the door.

The last several years had been hard for Jason. His father's unexplained death hung heavily in the household. The police inquiries determined that Mr. Preen accidentally transitioned to the afterlife trying to pull scrap lumber from the rafters in the garage. In any case, his mom still blamed her son for the loss.

Mrs. Preen bore her considerable weight to the hollow lauan door. The cheap latch gave way, and the woman crashed inward. Jason screamed, his eyelashes fluttering like butterflies. Running to the window, he tried leaping through the glass—not as easy as depicted in the movies.

Panting, his mother grabbed his bleeding legs and pulled the lad back inside. Furious, she proceeded to slap her son silly.

"You're sinful. You're an evil boy!" Mrs. Preen sputtered, her amber eyes spinning.

Jason scrambled for the exit. Mom was angry now—he could tell by the fire iron.

"Get over here you little bastard. I'm gonna pound your head in!" His mom came after him swinging the bent poker.

Jason cringed, but managed to grab the Barbie fashion doll hidden under his dresser. The toy was super sexy, especially with its alien figure. After school the juvenile used the figurine to study female anatomy.

"Damn you, damn you," Jason intoned, giving his mother the evil eye. The youth concentrated as he bashed the Barbie's head upon the doorframe. "Damn you! Damn you! Damn you!" he hollered, eyes hard as glittering stones.

Mrs. Preen staggered as her skin blanched. "AAAAIIIIEE-EEE!" she shrieked, gripping her temples. Swelling, his mother's head resembled a monstrous jack o' lantern.

Jason continued to whale on the diminutive Barbie. It was horrible (and awesome) to watch his mom's head explode.

Car Wash

I GOT A JOB AT THE LOCAL CAR WASH, learning that most people only get their vehicles cleaned on sunny days. My assignment is to dry the cars by hand using Turkish towels. If I am lucky, there might be a decent tip.

A super-long Winnebago camper pulled into the queue. Many stickers plastered the bumpers proclaiming the different places the family had traveled. The recreational vehicle looked too big to fit into the car wash, but I figured the cashier would turn the customer away.

When I pivoted, the jumbo RV could be seen inside the building, roller brushes whirling across the corrugated sides. Surprised that the humongous motorhome fit, a loud banging caught my ear. Fabricated of glass, the length of car wash afforded an unobstructed view of what occurred within. The entire structure filled with soapy water and fishes of various sizes swam throughout the shifting currents.

The father of the family pounded on the window trying to solicit my attention. I walked to the glass and with a finger, drew a happy face in the dew. As he tried to speak, prismatic bubbles fluttered upwards.

I repeated, "What? WHAT ARE YOU SAYING?" A yellow angelfish swam directly into the man's open yap.

My boss ordered me to continue drying the exiting automobiles. The towels were so wet and filthy, they made the cars dirtier.

A cigarette-smoking woman in a mud-streaked Chevy pressed her nose against the driver-side window. Coughing, her golden teeth fell onto the dashboard.

Once again, El Jefe yelled at me to get back to work.

The Messenger

THE ENCOUNTER BEGAN AS IN IMPULSE, a lark actually, but it wasn't as if I hadn't considered the act before.

On a crisp September morning, I emerged from Penn Station at precisely eight forty-five. There he stood on the damp street, all pumped up and completely insane.

This is what I witnessed: a homeless man shouting gibberish, cantillating really, at the commuters. I became immediately enamored by an individual so fierce and so self-sure. The beguiling fellow had a message for us—the unenlightened. Without hesitation, I named him: *Jesus.*

I was late for work watching the preacher, but didn't care. Nothing else downtown could top this show. Jesus wore multi-pocketed parachute pants stuffed with unknown objects, a dark blue Yankees sweatshirt and greasy, red Converse sneakers. A wild mane of blonde hair flowed along his spine.

The Messenger raised sacred scriptures up to Zion. By the Redeemer's raging posture, I understood the epistle was mighty important. At the top of his lungs, The Good Shepherd exhorted the same unintelligible words, high-pitched voice raw—ruined by constant abuse.

Intrigued, I listened, soliciting to understand the doctrine—impossible for a mere mortal. I remained torn. For ages, I wanted to talk to a schizophrenic, but was missing a mandatory meeting with my boss and besides—I felt afraid.

"What the hell," I said, with a rare devil-may-care mindset. Leaving my caffè latte on a newspaper vending machine, I crossed to the other side, ready to ask the Messiah a spiritual question and wholeheartedly interpret the answer.

Upon further review, I noticed that life had been unkind to this poor soul: pockmarked skin ravaged by disease, stained clothes hanging from a skeletal frame, and a big toe poking from a shoe. Within spitting distance, Jesus smelled like raw potatoes and shit.

Revitalized, I approached.

The Lamb of God's upturned eyes blazed into the sky—two powerful laser beams from heaven or hell held the secrets to everything.

"Buddy," I asked, "have you got the time?" I tensed, ready to defend myself.

The maniac on the Manhattan corner didn't blink an eye as he amplified the incessant raving.

"Hey, Jack!" I said louder and more demanding. "What time you got?"

The fool was deaf or simply ignoring me. It was also possible that he didn't even perceive I existed. Brazen, I braced myself, a small boy poking a stick in a beehive, hoping to get some action.

"Hey motherfucker!" I yelled. "What's the goddamn time?"

The man I christened Jesus turned to me, his countenance both alluring and repugnant. "Yes," the drifter said, weighing my soul, his eyes glassy, yet lucid. "True, I am a motherfucker. I am the son-of-a-bitch who fucked your sister Gail when she turned thirteen. It is me, the asshole who ran over your pet rabbit. The *kaninchen's* name was Hoppy, *korrekt?*"

Rapture enveloped me—darkness and light/pity and salvation.

"Father," I worshipped, falling to my knees. A searing pain coursed through my left arm ending deep in my chest.

A child tethered to a Mickey Mouse balloon stopped, mesmerized by a bum performing last rites to a businessman lying in the bus lane.

Dead Man Sings

"I SAW A DEAD MAN SING LAST NIGHT," Geoffrey informed Robert. The co-workers sat on a bench at the 14th Street station waiting for the PATH train to take them to Hoboken.

"Yeah, I heard something on that," Robert yawned, looking up from his *U.S. News*. "What's that all about, anyway?"

"Rob, it was pretty weird. They put a silicon chip in his head and propelled the body using a computer. I don't think the man literally sang. Probably lip-synced, but the illusion is nevertheless quite remarkable."

"How the hell did you get into that? I thought the show had been sold out. That was his funeral, right?" Snorting, Robert's snot rocket sizzled on the sidewalk.

"Yup. Peter over in marketing got a pair of tickets, but his girlfriend refused to go. She found the whole thing ethically macabre, so Pete let me buy them. The money was well worth it. I took Hilary from accounting, and she was very thankful, if you get what I mean." Geoffrey winked and puffed on a miniature cigar.

The well-loved operatic tenor had died during a coronary event four days after his seventy-third birthday. His manager arranged a final appearance utilizing Mortbotics™, a subsidiary of Walt Disney Productions.

Robert took another bite of the leftover tuna fish sandwich and mumbled, "Yeah, but how does the procedure actually work?"

Utilizing the Cigarillo butt, Geoffrey lit a joint and answered, "The concert's program had a good summarization on reanimation. The process is amazingly simple, although technologically intricate. A device is exploded in the deceased entertainer's cerebellum. Thousands of tinsel-shaped, micro-filaments become laced throughout the brain tissue, each connected to a central Oreo cookie-sized silicone chip. The unit links by wireless transmission to a mainframe host. I noticed two video cameras: one trained on the puppet and the other covering the puppeteer, who simultaneously controls the artist with his own actions. Preceding the concert, test signals are created by individually stimulating each micro-filament electrode. The camera digitally records each action of the cadaver."

As a PATH train came screeching to a halt, the suits sprinted to the packed railcar.

Geoffrey continued, "Each gesture is categorized and reprogrammed to duplicate every movement that the puppeteer pantomimes. Under close scrutiny, the motion is choppy, similar to watching an old silent movie, but at a distance, such as when performing on stage for an enthusiastic audience, the show is absolutely believable. During activation, the subject is given a highly-oxygenated blood transfusion to provide energy. This charge lasts thirty minutes, although longer-lasting recirculating liquid oxygen experiments are showing great promise. Even a properly prepared corpse is at most usable for three days before decomposition destroys muscle function."

Robert, jammed up against the sliding door inquired, "Wow, you certainly are well versed in Mortbotics™. Geoff, didn't it, you know, kind of stink?"

"Oh no, Rob," Geoffrey responded enthusiastically. "Passarelli is still an excellent tenor."

Dance

TYSON UNCOMFORTABLY LEANED against the back wall of the balloon-decorated gymnasium. He and the other geeks fidgeted watching their classmates bump and grind to the funky beat. The boy scratched the top of his head, attempting conversation with Bovac, the King of the Nerds.

As they discussed quantum theory, the teenager noticed a slender, dark-haired girl dancing sensuously to the captivating rhythm. Intimidated by Megan's radiance, his heart galloped up his throat in nervous excitement.

"Ralph?" Tyson questioned Bovac. "Have you ever danced with a girl?"

"What for?" Ralph answered with contempt. "Girls are stupid and full of germs. That reminds me, did you hear that MIT researchers have pioneered a revolutionary human protein template? It is alleged to be extremely accurate, even at high temperatures."

"No, I didn't know that," Tyson responded meekly. "I'm heading to the boy's room. See you later."

The lad made his way to the lavatory located on the far end of the gym. He discreetly kept out of everyone's way, although he accidentally trampled on one wild dancer's toes.

At the sink, Tyson splashed cool water across his cheeks as the other boys joked and smoked. Squinting, the teenager studied his gaunt reflection, looking for any signs of handsomeness. There were none to be seen on the pimply mug. In despair, the adolescent grabbed a handful of paper towels and dried his face.

"Hey Weasel," a tall, narrow-eyed, senior slurred. "Are ya gonna get any tonight?"

The bathroom crowd hooted crazily at the hysterical comment. Tyson blushed and scurried from the stinky room.

Outside, the party was jumping. It seemed to Tyson that everyone was either dancing closely or making-out in the corners. His heart skipped seeing the woman of his dreams standing alone by the punch bowl.

"I've got to make my move," the juvenile murmured, planning his actions. "If I don't do this now, I'll never, ever, get any."

Tyson approached the beauty, his lower lip twitching uncontrollably. The girl saw him coming and her eyes locked on his.

"Would you like to dance, Megan?" the foolish schoolboy asked.

"No, I don't dance with freaks," God's Gift to Mankind replied, as she scooted around him and escaped to her friends

Tyson stood quietly for a moment before leaving the building. As the rejected youth peddled the stolen banana bike home, tears of loneliness streamed down his face.

Cycling faster and faster, Tyson's emotions soon turned to rage. "Bitch, bitch, bitch," he chanted in cadence to the whir of his tires. "That bitch is gonna pay!"

T-Bone

IT WAS HARD TO GUESS how many hours Blaine Horton lay there. From the heavens, the stars were the sole points of reference in the utter blackness. The man lay in a ditch, a deep refuse-filled channel. A trickle of effluent flowed between the musician's shoulder blades, to the small of his back, and through the crack in his ass. Dank, but somehow womb-like reassuring, Blaine hoped the tepid fluid was water rather than his own blood.

Gloria had ordered him to get out. "Get out, asshole!"

"What are you nuts?" Blaine asked, eyes glued to the revolver's barrel and Gloria's twitching fingers. "I'm sorry," he pleaded, beginning to realize the woman was serious.

"Get the fuck out of the car, you creep!" the schoolteacher shrilled. She raised the gun up to Blaine's face, poking him in the forehead. The passenger swung the Ford's door and plunged into the darkness, attempting to protect his head with tucked arms. Tumbling along at sixty miles per hour, the band leader glimpsed Gloria stretching over to slam the Pinto's door shut. The dome light went out.

Earlier in the evening, Blaine grabbed Gloria's breast.

After leaving the bar, Gloria chatted incessantly about her second grade students. Bored by a lengthy diatribe detailing a foiled milk-money caper, Blaine watched Gloria's chest bounce in the green glow of the instrument panel. Copping a feel on a first date was considered standard for an up and coming rock star.

The bushes rustled in the distance—the first sound Blaine had noticed. This was a remote road and he predicted many lonely hours before another car passed.

The aging mongrel of contrasting heritage and numerous human names was on the hunt. The cur had eaten sporadically during the last few days, mostly from garbage cans or the occasional road kill. Much of this dreck he vomited, leaving the canine as hungry as ever. The last raw meat had been nearly a week ago, a ground hog that looked the wrong way upon emerging from his burrow. The lingering memory of sweet flesh hastened T-Bone's (his previous owner was a butcher) pace. Following the fresh trail of a male feline musk, a string of saliva hung from the curled lips.

The man lay flat on his spine, feet extended and arms resting by his sides. Blaine systematically checked for injuries in the dim starlight. The pant legs were torn and one Timberland moccasin was missing—the sock dark with mud *or blood.*

Wanting to test his legs, he was afraid they wouldn't work so he tried to move the fingers of his right hand. The digits unclasped slowly, as if by remote control. Blaine tried to raise his right arm—agony more excruciating than he could believe wracked his shoulder. He let the battered limb splash into the stream. Now for his left. Again he tried moving the fingers, this time feeling zilch. Craning his neck, Blaine shrieked when he saw the mangled limb. Grey nothingness descended upon the man in the gutter.

T-Bone's ears pricked up when he heard the escalating yowls. Wary but curious, the starving hound homed in on the noise. Blaine's trench drained into the very stream T-Bone drank from. The coppery water on T-Bone's tongue tasted of man. Famished, he quickened his gate.

Blaine lay semi-conscious, dreaming of heart surgery. Mork, a fat-jowled tom lay upon his chest, sucking oxygen from the injured man's nostrils. The cat kneaded the performer's ribs, claws rhythmically opening and closing.

Hunched in the stream, T-Bone inhaled. In the water ahead, a feline perched upon a sleeping human. The tabby licked the man's face and lay his head down. T-Bone charged the pair.

Mork, alerted by the rushing water leapt from Blaine's chest, nails gaining traction in the soft skin. The singer awoke with an outcry, finding a growling beast ready to pounce.

"Stay away devil dog!" Blaine screamed.

The Accident

JIMMY BAXTER HAD DIFFICULTY maneuvering himself across the classroom. The three foot section of iron railing protruding from his forehead was cumbersome and impaired peripheral vision. Jimmy's neck twisted obliquely as the metal bar sparked against the blackboard.

"Sit down Jimmy!" Sister Marjorie ordered. "You are disrupting the class."

The frustrated tadpole angrily stomped to his school desk, tired of lugging about the sixty pound hunk of rebar.

Recess was no longer enjoyable. "Get away! Get off!" Baxter shouted to the laughing children hanging from his manmade antlers.

"Oh, shut up, Jungle Jim!" Skittles teased in Jimmy's ear.

Jimmy had been a normal boy until the afternoon his grandpa accidentally dropped him off the front stoop.

"Yippie-yi-yo-ki-yay," the senior citizen hooted as he excitedly whirled the seven-year-old whippersnapper around his head. "Whoops," Gramps giggled as feeble fingers slipped from his favorite grandson's sweaty ankles.

The half-pint winged over the garden, his head impaling onto the rusty gate. Frantic bawling alerted his mother to this new dilemma.

"Oh, my Lord! Dad, you old fool!" Mrs. Baxter chided, praying the neighbors had not seen. "I warned you not to roughhouse."

"Lady, we'll kill him if we pull his noggin off that fence," Rocco the mailman advised. "The doctors will figure out what to do," he promised, his breath reeking of onions and garlic.

The ambulance arrived promptly. Following standard procedures, the paramedics used the Jaws of Life to cut away the section of fence penetrating Jimmy's brow.

The hospital was also unwilling to take responsibility for pulling the spike from the child's cranium. "He should grow out of it sooner or later, Mrs. Baxter," the specialists informed Jimmy's disgruntled mother.

Wild Bill's Workshop

THE CHEVY SCRAPED THE CURB in front of Classic Beverages.

"Jeez! Can't you do anything right, dumbass?" Wild Bill hissed at his partner.

"What?" Marty Fastbender grumbled, scanning the neighborhood.

"You'd better be here when I come out. Just don't fuck this up. Got it?"

Wild Bill peered through the vivid neon tubing into the liquor store. The establishment appeared to be empty except for the owner, his head hidden behind a flashing Coors Silver Bullet sign. Under a streetlight, the robber double-checked his piece, a cheap Chinese 9mm automatic. The clip only contained four shells—they would have to be enough. Wild Bill worked a slug into the chamber and placed the gun in his waistband.

"Ready or not, here I come," the bandit murmured, giving Marty a final glare.

Wild Bill hitched his dungarees and stretched in the multicolored glow. The street remained deserted at seven minutes to eleven o'clock—the liquor store about to close. He slid the weapon into a recent copy of the Daily News.

Richard Fand glanced up as the bells on the glass door jingled. Expressionless, he monitored the nondescript man wearing a 49'ers cap, plaid shirt and blue jeans. Clutching a newspaper, the customer walked to the rear. Ricky stared out the window and noticed a man waiting in a souped-up Camaro. As they locked eyes, the driver turned away. Now the fellow stood by the refrigerators, his narrowed eyes reflecting in the glass.

Frowning, Ricky reached for his 12-gauge sawed-off shotgun.

Marty had trouble breathing with the sock jammed deep into his throat. His left nostril became clogged with mucus and he wanted to sneeze, but was afraid he might choke.

Strapped to a support beam in Wild Bill's cellar, the getaway driver's arms were snugly attached to the cross member with U-bolts.

Fastbender's head was jammed between the rafters. Protruding nails from the upper level's floorboards drastically reduced movement. Stacked Wawa milk crates supported his bound feet. Sawdust carpeted the concrete.

Wild Bill stood before the secured man, a bare bulb swinging overhead. From the light fixture an orange twenty-foot extension cord snaked to the cement, looped into coils and up again into his hand. The southpaw gripped a Sears electric drill.

"That was quite a haul, eh pal?" Wild Bill questioned, gesturing to the stack of bills piled on the Sears Craftsman table saw. "Four hundred and fifty-two smackers. Ain't that some shit? I'd like to give you your half—but I don't think so. Marty, I need that bread, I really do. It's for a worthy cause too. Wild Bill needs a band saw. I can't make curved cuts with this circular saw, and my portable saber saw isn't powerful enough for furniture-grade hardwood. Hold on a sec—let me get the catalogue and show you."

Wild Bill slid open a shiny file cabinet crammed full of paper.

"I keep my catalogues in here. Tools mostly, but I do have several electronics brochures and a couple from J.C. Whitney. Take a gander," Wild Bill urged, fishing out the latest Sears mailer. The crook paged to the power tool section and revealed a grey and red Craftsman band saw. "Nice, huh?" he asked, holding the circled image up to his captive's face. Marty nodded imperceptibly, avoiding the three-inch rusty nail that tickled his eyelash.

Ricky Fand sprawled in a pool of blood. "I'm not as quick as I used to be," the liquor store owner groaned, rolling onto his side. Several years earlier, the NRA member had bulls-eyed two looters during a black-out.

Dizzy and weak, Ricky hauled himself up to the counter. Belt removed, he cinched a tourniquet above the wound. Having seen Zeke Anderson save a wounded soldier on the CBS series *Tour of Duty*, Fand was mighty relieved to see that the technique stemmed the flow. Propped against the glass, wondering how the stickup artist had gotten the drop on him, Ricky focused upon a wallet on the floor halfway to the exit.

Now alone, Marty strove to get loose, but could not. Scared, he blew his nose onto his chin and wet himself.

"Hallelujah!" Wild Bill yelled, swerving to hit a crow pecking an ironed opossum. A carton containing a Sears Craftsman band saw slid across the rear seat of his hatchback. The radio blasted a classic Frank Sinatra tune.

The seat of Ricky's Toyota was sticky with blood, but he didn't care. Fand wanted payback—and he damn sure was gonna get it. The former sheriff drove faster.

Marty gave up trying to get loose. Listening to cars whizz by outside, he frantically waited to hear a specific car door slam. The taste of his sock was a bitter treat.

Wild Bill pulled into his driveway. "The trim will need painting," he mused. "There'll be time to do that in the fall." He yanked the cardboard box onto the macadam and went to get the hand truck in the garage. Rolling up the door, Wild Bill stared down the chopped barrel of a shotgun.

"Turn around, William Turner," Ricky ordered.

The man looked serious, so Wild Bill obeyed. The robber shuddered in surprise as the steel bucket of high-test motor fuel encased his head, blind to the flash of the "NASCAR" Bic lighter. As Mr. Turner danced around the billowing garage, Ricky scooped the band saw onto the hand truck and wheeled the tool over to his pickup. Grimacing, he hoisted the tool into the bed and sped away.

Marty heard his partner screaming outside. Barely able to shift his eyeballs, he watched a burning figure run past the basement window. Upstairs, Wild Bill's woodworking projects were consumed by the fire storm. Shortly thereafter, Marty's hairpiece exploded into flames.

The Interview

BRET TAYLOR TAPPED HIS FINGERS waiting for the receptionist to say his name. Nervous, he grabbed a *New England Today* magazine and flipped the pages, barely glancing at the glossy illustrations of rickety covered bridges and ramshackle barns. Taylor sweated profusely, his armpits rank with pre-interview funk. The pudgy unemployed man winged the periodical onto the table, scattering the gossip tabloids.

"Christ," Bret muttered, impatiently standing and shuffling to the window. A crew of garbage men kibitzing on the corner temporarily held his interest. "How come they have a job?" he wondered, observing the rush-hour traffic. Frowning, his stomach lurched reliving his "resignation."

Taylor screwed up the McCartney deal. Not only did the firm lose its biggest account to their largest rival, Bret had made his boss, Joe Strummer look like a buffoon.

"Get out, get out!" Joe had rumbled. "Get your crap and get lost, you stupid ass!" Eyes bulging, his boss heaved a cigarette-laden ashtray at Bret's head. "And don't come back!"

"I quit," Bret stammered as he rode the elevator to the street.

By the time the drunken man arrived home that night, he had rehearsed a statement for his wife: "Honey, I'm glad I quit that hellhole. This way I can get a real job. And I'll be able to buy that drop top Beamer you always wanted."

Bret's mind returned to reality hearing his name.

"Mr. Taylor, we're ready for you now," the receptionist beckoned.

As Bret followed the robotic worker through aisles of cubicles, he tried not to think of himself as a complete loser. After a while, they arrived in a dark and dirty corridor behind the elevator shafts.

"Mr. Babikov has been anxious to meet you, Mr. Taylor," the clerk confided as they maneuvered around piles of archaic office machinery.

They stepped into a cramped storeroom and introductions were made. The lingering stench of urine and cleaning supplies tickled Bret's nose.

"Sit here, Mr. Taylor," the fat man lisped. "May I call you Bret?" The interviewee nodded and sat on a sagging cardboard box. "Tell me about yourself." Dark penetrating eyes evaluated his three-piece suit. It was oppressively stuffy in the janitor's closet.

"Sir, I have a PhD in Business Management from Harvard and was Vice President in charge of domestic and foreign accounts at IBM for nineteen years. I was born in northern New Jersey and have a wife and two children. Mr. Babikov, I really need this job and I'll do anything to get it. You'll get a hard worker. I swear I won't let you down! Please Mr. Babikov!" the out of work man jabbered.

Mr. Babikov turned away in disgust. A timecard clock ticked in rhythm with the dripping water.

Taylor knew that he would not get this job. He had been on many interviews and could tell when he wasn't wanted.

"Bret, let me see your hands," Mr. Babikov directed.

Startled, Bret shoved his trembling fists into the other man's face.

Mr. Babikov stretched on white silk gloves and meticulously read Bret's palms, principally studying the fingernails.

"Bret you are overqualified for the job I had in mind, but we do need someone on a temporary basis. Follow me please."

Boss and employee went into the junk-filled outer area. Yards of typewriters and file cabinets disappeared into the distance.

"Clean up all this shit and I'll give you twenty bucks," Mr. Babikov commanded.

Fifteen Miscellaneous and Unrelated Statements

1. The three men from Honduras acclimated to the frigid conditions in the meat locker.
2. Upon handling the armadillo, Nancy's skin became toad-like.
3. The donation of porcelain reamers was made possible by a massive grant from the Proctor Silex Corporation.
4. The lobster boat used to have graceful lines.
5. Please do not touch things that you should not.
6. Trent still felt randy and unsatisfied.
7. The dead man's pockets revealed nothing of interest.
8. My mother wasted years knitting unwanted gifts.
9. After the date, Skip remained unsure how to safely dispose of the Popsicle stick.
10. On Friday, I have a lunch appointment to have a boil lanced.
11. Many nooses hung from the trees of the trailer court.
12. Not everyone has the same number of teeth in their mouth.
13. Two weeks ago, I lost my most valued possession.
14. I never tasted rancid butter; therefore I served the oily paddies to my guests.
15. It was a long walk home after Mommy dumped me from the car.

Freezers

TYSON WRAPPED THE ARTICLE with wax paper and sighed. "Christ, I'm running out of space again," he grumbled, precisely taping the seam prior to sliding the package into the tiny freezer.

The dwelling was crammed with freezers, twenty-three, to be precise. During the last seven years, the meat packer had dragged a collection of iceboxes up onto the porch and into his cottage. Located in Clifton, New Jersey, the house was chocked-full of coolers. Some had been purchased new using the Sears credit card, while others were bought used in the industrial section of town. Occasionally, a decent unit could be found on the curb on trash day, just waiting for Tyson's skilled hands to recondition.

Today, he stocked the General Electric chest situated in the bathroom. The nine cubic inch unit was stacked on top of a full-size Whirlpool model. Tyson closed the door and studied the chart fastened with carrot magnets. Cryptically he filled in and initialed the appropriate columns.

The hoarding initiated after a bungled date rape. Marsha Tate, Tyson's rendezvous for the evening, upset him when she resisted his amorous advances. "Be quiet, please shut up!" Tyson had pleaded as he pounded her head against the Chevy

Malibu's window. "Jeez, why did you have to fuss, Marsha?" the sad sack carped.

Not knowing what to do, Tyson took the dead girl home. The slaughterer came up with a plan after hours of staring at her body propped against the kitchen refrigerator. Employing basic cooking implements, the woman's body easily came apart under his attentive dissection.

Wise to the dangers of freezer burn, Tyson devised an intricate method of preservation. First, he prepared the surface by scrubbing the subject's skin with soap and water. Then he rubbed in hand cream, usually Jergens. A heavy application of Vaseline liberally coated all nooks and crannies, followed by yards of Saran Wrap (sprayed with Lysol Disinfectant). Finally, a layer of Reynolds Wrap Aluminum Foil gave the whole figure a shiny space-age look. The females were meticulously labeled: name, age, weight, eye color and date.

Tyson wasn't smooth with women and before long his house was filled with freezers.

Colony

TABOR GENTLY GROOMED Queen Tahmoor's head. Her glazed compound eyes were flecked with specks of microscopic fungi.

In another section of the Ant Farm, Tutu labored with a task of his own. The western harvester frantically scurried to and fro lugging a colossal grasshopper leg. Tutu's sturdy exoskeleton effortlessly supported the hefty limb.

Tabor's stomach grumbled, but he couldn't go to the Food Room until he finished sprucing up the Queen. Tahmoor was Queen of the Ants after all.

Tabor's miniscule ant brain vaguely remembered the terrible flood. Unbeknownst to him (or the rest of the colony), a young third grade student named Dwight had poured a neon cup of SunnyD into the Ant Farm's main entrance hatch. Sensing impending doom, Tabor and Tutu scrambled to the Queen's throne room residing deep in the bowels of the subterranean world.

"Squeak-squawk!" Tabor shouted as he galloped around and around, back and forth, and up and down the walls of the chamber.

"Tweak-twawk!" Tutu bellowed, his plated abdomen quivering.

Queen Tahmoor, deep in thought laying eggs, ignored the worker ants and continued rubbing her aching thorax. Tabor heroically grabbed the Queen and pulled her hulking frame toward the only exit. Tutu pushed the Queen's big backside.

The Queen was massive, a giant ant if you will. Tabor backed through first, as Tutu forced the Queen into the narrow opening. Tahmoor was way too big, but a measly two hundred fifty thousand brain neurons could not possibly deduce that. Strong Tutu shoved, all six legs kicking up boulders of sand as he desperately tried to rescue the Queen.

Five long minutes later, the Queen's stately head broke off her jointed body. Tabor was at fault, yanking too hard on the Queen's elbowed antennae with his powerful mandibles. As the *Pogonomyrmex occidentalis* crashed backwards into a tunnel shaft, the noggin chased him like an oversized beach ball. After the dust settled and Tutu left in a panic, Tabor commenced his frantic cleaning session.

As Mrs. Milton's giggling pupils pressed their runny noses against the scratched plastic of the Ant Farm, the teacher informed her class that ants are not very bright.

Huffy

FRANKIE PRECISELY ATTACHED the playing cards to the bicycle's tubular frame. Applying clothespins, he adjusted the stiff papers until they just touched the wheel's spokes. *Perfect!* The boy always used Queens in the front and Kings in the back.

Now his machine was complete. The brand-new 1966 Huffy was painted fire red with green pin stripes. Additionally, the Silver Jet had three gears in the rear hub and a loud electric horn mounted in the crotch bar. The two-wheeler was a beaut. Frankie pushed off, rolling out of his garage and down the driveway.

Gliding on one peddle, he whipped into the street before swinging his lanky leg over the seat to begin his journey. Handlebars firmly gripped, Frankie raised and peddled furiously. Damien, his best friend lived on the other side of town in what Frank's mom nicknamed "ghettoville."

Approaching the hill, the youth leaned past the handlebars, pressing even harder, the playing cards rumbling loud as a throaty V-8. This was Frank's favorite part (unless he was riding home), a long winding run that allowed the lad to build up tremendous speed. Tears streaked from his baby blues as the Firestone Champions stuck to the asphalt like glue.

Fifty yards downhill, Jane's bare legs obstructed the bike lane. The kidnapped girl's face and upper torso remained concealed with autumn leaves.

"Yee-ha!" Frankie whooped, as he approached the new obstacle. "Go for the shins," the teenager breathed, readying for the hurdle.

The master rider yanked the Huffy up off the blacktop at exactly the right instant; only leaving slight tread imprints on Jane's swollen ankles.

Later that day, recounting his story to Damien, Frankie wondered if his mom could be convinced to buy silver streamers for the ends of his handlebars.

Devil's Corridor

CLIFF GLANCED IN THE SIDE MIRROR as his decrepit Ford bounced along Route 17 South.

"Goddamn. How could I have been so stupid? Dear God please help me," Cliff prayed through clenched teeth. "I'll never do that again."

The puny brush salesman had cutoff a Cadillac on the giant clover leaf at Route 4. Now the powerful road locomotive was after him. Cliff stomped the pedal and held on. The economy shit-box lurched over the rutted "Devil's Corridor," a narrow potholed stretch of highway with few, if any shoulders. At the raucous blaring of his pursuer's horn, he winced in the bucket seat, almost sideswiping the wheels of an enormous semi.

They were after him—three burley rednecks, probably released from jail. Images of rape flashed through Cliff's mind and he involuntarily clutched his buttock cheeks.

"I hope I don't run out of gas!" Cliff thought, checking the needle of the fuel gauge nestled amongst the idiot lights. The indicator was below E—in the danger zone. Behind the eyeglasses, the salesman's eyes buggered as his mind searched for the last time he had filled up.

The right side of the highway was gridlocked with cars and trucks making the fast lane Cliff's best bet. In the rear-view mirror, the land yacht appeared to be on his bumper—the thick-shouldered driver leaning through the rear window. Cursing, the man flashed the finger.

Cliff turned his head forward, just in time to see the stopped I-beam truck with the flashing warning lights. The red safety rag hit our protagonist's forehead first, softening the effect of twenty-six tons of cold-rolled steel.

Hairless

HOWARD TUTTLE WATCHED a lot of television. At bedtime he could not sleep. This latest bout of insomnia was exhausting. Night after restless night tossing and turning really was a drag.

This evening began with repetitive chores, followed by a series of boring sitcoms. By nine thirty, Howard's eyelids drooped. At eleven o'clock, he hauled himself out of the armchair to crawl upstairs to his dismal bedroom. On the sagging mattress, the man quietly waited for the crazy thoughts and visions that generally preceded sleep. *Nothing!* For the previous three weeks, Tuttle's mind remained crystal clear thinking about smooth skin.

The phobia/fetish started at the barber shop when he noticed an article in *Vogue* magazine on hair removal. The piece was intriguingly titled "Happy Hairless Summer Fun!!!" The author described various depilation methods necessary for sexy swimsuit wear.

This returned the memory of a story Howard heard at the foundry regarding a woman that had *absolutely* no hair on any part of her body. Turned on to the point of shaking, this fantasy popped into the machinist's mind at the most inopportune moments.

Tuttle found himself studying women more closely—checking their levels of hirsuteness. It disgusted him seeing the wisps of female fur coating the backs of elongated necks or the blonde peach fuzz covering slender arms. Howard hated hair.

Giving in at 3:30 a.m., the insomniac turned on the idiot box. A commercial showing long-legged, bikini-clad girls prancing in front of a fake volleyball net intrigued him. As the ad concluded, a giant pink bottle of Nair filled the screen.

"That's it," Howard moaned. "I want a gal with no hair, no hair at all."

The problem was that Tuttle didn't have a girlfriend and had never been in a relationship.

"I gots to get me some of that stuff for *her*," Howard told the reflection in the bathroom mirror. "I'm gonna get that Nair for *her*."

Howard grabbed his windbreaker and headed into the dawn. In the barrio, he stopped the Chevy Vega at an open bodega. Under unflattering fluorescence, the lathe operator stood in the personal hygiene section. There was no Nair; however there were two Honeycomb Waxing Kits. Overjoyed, Tuttle shoved one in his jacket and paid for the other at the register.

In his bathroom, Howard studied the directions. Although awfully complicated, he felt he had the wherewithal to complete the task.

The initial step was to heat the beeswax in the miniature crock pot. Next, you applied the melted concoction to "the selected folliculated body parts" with the supplied wooden spatula. Licking the birch stick, Howard was reminded of the vanilla cups he bought as a schoolboy from the ice cream truck. Before the sticky goo cooled, you slapped on a layer of gauze. The machinist swabbed the wax on his arm and pressed down the cloth.

"Yip, yip, yippee!" Tuttle yipped, yanking the strip from his arm. After the tears dried, he witnessed lovely, smooth, unsullied epidermis.

"Hair ain't fair, ain't fair, no hair, no hair," Howard sang as he epilated the rest of his body.

Mother

Mother asked me to take out the garbage, late last night,
"Don't dilly, don't dally. Make sure you do it right."
I sighed as I vacated the corner of my room,
I prayed the end of my punishment might come soon.
In the electric gleam of the linoleum—so new,
I tripped over my big, clumsy school shoes.
Coffee grounds a terrible mess,
flew like a sparrow onto Mom's new church dress.
"Goddamn you, goddamn you!" she was heard to say.
"You won't live to see another day!"

Skinny Puppy

SKINNY PUPPY WAS ON THE PROWL, the prowl for food that is. Alone in this big and dangerous world, Skinny Puppy's indifferent mother and two identical half-wit brothers had been sent to dog heaven by a Chevy Chevette—the runt's lagging gate being the only thing that saved him from oblivion. Now the pup's days were filled with the endless search for sustenance.

Skinny Puppy was a German Shepherd. Well not really. His father had been a German Shepherd and his mother had been a mangy, brown bitch of indeterminate heritage. The mutt's growing paws indicated he'd ultimately be a gigantic dog.

Right now, the starving beast wandered about an alley behind Roy's Family Diner, a rundown eatery a couple blocks from the Atlantic Ocean. Roy's brand of fatty fried cooking accounted for the many undigested meals residing in the trash cans out back—tip-top eating for the neighborhood rodent, feral canine and feline populations.

Tonight, the animal smelled the unmistakable raw stench of human wafting from a tin garbage pail. The odor was not the usual scent that normally adorned the handles and paper debris filling the container. This offal had a stronger flavor, somehow richer.

As the dog tipped the can over, rubbish cascaded onto the greasy macadam. Mostly, the refuse was just paper and plastic, but a few ketchup-soaked French fries and a jar of contaminated mayonnaise momentarily held his attention. *What are those tempting objects wrapped in tin foil?* Skinny Puppy ripped the packages open and gorged himself on: *Marsha Tate, 23, 135 lbs., blue eyes, 03/18/1983.*

Sinucrabs

A Science Paper by Jerold Gao

I discovered the cause of the common cold, and have devised a cure. The benefits to mankind will be immeasurable.

July 14, 1990

On this evening, I went to sleep utterly spent. In the shadows, I feverishly tossed and turned, strange hallucinations filling my mind. The next morning, I awoke with a sore throat. The daytime brought even more symptoms: runny nose, swollen uvula, itchy eyes and a general feeling of malaise.

July 15-20, 1990

During this period, the illness progressed to a state where my nose became totally clogged with yellow/green mucus, making breathing laborious. I was very tired and depressed.

July 21, 1990

This forenoon brought new hope. A stuffy woman in a television commercial said, "Sinutab." My plugged ears heard, "Sinucrab."

"What if," I conjectured, "there are crabs living in my sinus cavities? What if it is their excrement dripping from my nose?" These are just a few of the revealing notions that bounced through my febrific mind.

July 23, 1990

I am at the coughing stage of my malady. Every few minutes, I burst into phlegm-flying hacking fits. Between these spells, I work on my thesis. Here is an early outline of the research:

1. Sinuses are Caves in the Head
    a. Sinucrabs Live in these Moist Grottos
2. Sinucrabs are Tiny Microscopic Organisms
    a. They Resemble Crabs
        i. Ugly
        ii. No Eyes (nocturnal)
        iii. Have Pinchers (bloody nose)
3. Sinucrabs Excrete Much Waste
    a. Waste is Mucus
        i. Liquid discharge Irritates Eyes and Throat (acidity)
        ii. Solid Feces is Thick and Green
4. Sinucrabs Feed on Blood (parasitic)
    a. This Accounts for Lethargy and Dizziness

July 24, 1990

I am now ingesting copious doses of codeine to relieve my cough. Cognitive faculties degenerating, I realized that this drug does not cure anything—the opiates merely mellow out the Sinucrabs. Bit by bit, I identified how Sinucrabs truly operate.

1. Sinucrabs Mate Like Crazy
    a. They Can't Help It!
2. Sinucrabs have a Limited Life-Span

   a. A Typical Sinucrab Lives Three Weeks (average time for rhinopharyngitis)
3. Sinucrabs Lay Millions of Eggs
   a. Eggs are Released from the Body Along with Sinucrab Droppings (infection)
      i. Eggs are Deposited in Environment
         1. Sneezing
         2. Coughing
         3. Spitting
         4. Puking
         5. Etc.
4. Sinucrab Eggs enter Victims' Sinuses
   a. Hands in Mouth
   b. Touching Eyes
   c. Picking Nose
   d. Kissing
   e. Etc.
5. Sinucrabs have a 24 Hour Gestation Period
   a. Eggs Hatch and Reproduce Immediately
6. Sinucrab Population Ultimately Drowns in its own Feces

July 28, 1990

I contemplated cures for Sinucrabs. Up until now, the solitary method to get over a cold was to wait for the Sinucrab populace to die out. As a boy, my father often took me crabbing at Point Pleasant, New Jersey. Tonight, I must devise miniature crab traps that can be nasally inserted.

July 30, 1990

The traps are ready and I am preparing to go crabbing.

Eighty-One Cents

FROM A DISTANCE, Arthur Craig saw his dad sitting on the stoop of their Brooklyn brownstone. Arthur and his younger sister Kay had just rounded the corner at the north end of Fountain Avenue, a lovely tree-lined street in a middle-class neighborhood. The children both held double-scoop ice cream cones. Arthur enthusiastically gobbled rocky mountain road. Kay's black raspberry spotted her white dress. The youths were returning from Carl's Ice Cream Parlor, where the owner served the treats with a toothy smile and best wishes.

Snug as two bugs in a rug, the pair strolled along the lane, eagerly slurping the melting cones. *This afternoon is so hot you could fry a robin's egg on your forehead*, Arthur thought. Earlier, he had heard that cliché and repeated the phrase skipping over cracks in the sidewalk. The schoolboy was still too immature to fashion a novel opinion.

As usual, Kay giggled, the cone waving dangerously as she gestured wildly. Arthur used his tongue to corral the leaking brown ice cream into his mouth.

Their dad sat motionless on the top step. Able Craig stared straight ahead, arms resting on his knees, hands clasped. The man seemed to be praying, which was unusual. Mr. Craig was not overly religious. As Arthur and Kay crossed the street, the boy noticed the family cat vigorously rubbing against his father's foot. Bejesus rotated his head to an upside-down position and spit-shined the wing-tipped shoes.

Bejesus had received his peculiar name from Mrs. Craig. Kay spotted the stray energetically covering its scat in the backyard sandbox. Afraid that her mother might not go for the idea of a pet, the child snuck the raggedy feline into her room, keeping the animal hidden for five days. Curious, Mrs. Craig investigated the maturing stench emanating from her daughter's bedroom. Kay's mom got a big surprise when she opened the closet.

"It scared the bejesus out of me," Mrs. Craig had informed Mr. Craig.

"Let's call him, Bejesus!" Arthur blurted.

"Splendid suggestion," Mr. Craig agreed proudly, smashing a walnut with the nutcracker his son gave him for Christmas.

"What a good kitty, Daddy!" Kay shouted across the street.

Mr. Craig looked up, his red-rimmed eyes widening and lower lip dropping as if to reply. Thirty-four Lincoln pennies spilled from his lips.

"Mommy's gone!" Kay shrieked. Forty-seven more cents gushed from the man's orifice as he pointed up the street.

Arthur stopped, dubious that his mother really left him, although knowing full well that his father wouldn't be sitting there with a mouth full of copper if she hadn't.

A Peterbilt truck thundered down upon the children. With a ten-year-old's keen reflexes, Arthur sprang backwards. Kay's unfinished dessert sailed as she accepted the full impact of the semi's chromed bumper.

Mr. Craig's wife never did reappear and this did not surprise anyone. Arthur learned a valuable lesson concerning the realities of superstition that humid June afternoon. Later in the week, little Kay was interred at Salem Fields Cemetery wearing the same bleached and starched dress.

To this day, Bejesus is still unaware of the worriment of men.

Saturn

SKIN PEELED SWIFTLY from my welted muscles. I was left naked, exposed.

A fellow with a similar tortured demeanor rubbed filth upon his glistening ribcage. "Try this!" the familiar man exclaimed, holding out a beaker containing fresh mung. "It's better than nothing, I guess."

I looked away from his disfigurement, hopeful I was not altogether so terrible.

The bare tendons in my skeletal hand clenched three spheres. Unable to release the rigor mortis grip, I slammed my wrist against a tomb. The globes fell from my fingers. The pain was refreshing and kept me conscious for a while longer. On all fours, I sniffed the orbs. The first was a marble, the second a ball bearing, the last a cracked eyeball.

"Jesus Christ!" I barked skywards. "Is this the Holy Trinity I've been hearing so much about?"

I flipped on my back, wanting my belly rubbed. A young boy holding a rolled up newspaper vaulted from a sycamore tree. "You've been bad. Very disobedient," he scolded raising the tumefied Sunday edition of the *New York Times*. I scampered onto the road.

An American-made Saturn sedan (featuring dent-resistant plastic body panels) broadsided me. Winded, I reached for my flattened hindquarters.

Hooting and hollering, I proclaimed, "I believe I broke my bloody arse!" I collected the shattered teeth with the dustpan helpfully provided by my local fan club.

"Well done! Bravo!" the crowd cheered, holding up gigantic placards to score my daring performance.

Cookout

ME AND ARTY WENT GONZO on the old guy. Arty hit all around the legs and feet with a bar of iron. I mainly booted the dude in the face. Busted him bad.

We beat Big Joe up pretty good and then Arty says, "I want to finish him off."

I say, "Be my guest."

Arty says, "Thanks, don't mind if I do," and takes out the lighter fluid that he always keeps and squirts the shit on Big Joe.

"Don't forget his hair," I say.

"His mop so greasy—forget about it," says Arty.

Arty lights the son-of-a-bitch and fire shoots out. I lean back a ways, but return to the heat. Fuckin' cold and I hold my hands out over Big Joe. He moans some, but I kick in his teeth and he shuts right up.

Arty says, "You hungry?"

I say, "Yeah brother. I'm hungry."

Gift of Love

A MAN LOVED A WOMAN. The romanticist's love was very strong, so he peeled the skin from his own back and tailored a handbag using hair for thread. A collar bone made a nice handle.

The woman accepted his token, but placed it high upon a shelf in the darkest depths of her closet. Turning, she promptly forgot the gift existed.

"I made you a beautiful handbag from my skin, hair, and bone. Why do you never use it?" the man whined, tears streaming down his face.

The woman became angry. "Only a fool would create such a hideous thing!"

Thievery

DON WIPED THE BLOOD from his buck knife onto the dead marshal's pants. My partner's face held no smile as we went for the gold.

The ancient stagecoach jerked as the horses panicked against the harnesses. An iron chest waited under the seat, protected by another corpse. We tossed the gut-shot deputy into the chaparral.

I did not trust Don in the least and awaited his betrayal. The box fell to the ground, the lock not withstanding a pickaxe. Up close, the coins were dazzling and Don used this moment to make his move.

"José, I'm sorry," he apologized.

Don hesitated, so I lunged for the Colt. The bandit fired into my screaming mouth—the bullet punching a thumb-sized hole in my cheek before heading into the desert. Like schoolboys, we grappled in the dust until I gained possession of the firearm. Putting the gun to Don's head, I laid my only friend to rest.

I packed the gold into the horse's saddle bags and headed south. It felt nice to be finally free of Don.

www.ingramcontent.com/pod-product-compliance
Lightning Source LLC
Chambersburg PA
CBHW020617120726
47905CB00003B/834

* 9 7 8 0 9 9 1 4 2 4 8 4 9 *